OIL SPILL

OIL SPILL

SIX SHORT STORIES

JOHN HOFFMAN

A SIFTING PRESS BOOK

SP-01

OIL SPILL

Copyright © 2024 John Hoffman

ISBN: 979-8-9914584-0-5 (Paperback)

This is a work of fiction. Names, characters, business, events, and incidents are the products of the author's imagination. Any resemblance to actual persons, living or dead, or actual events is purely coincidental.

Set in Genitium Basic type.
Copyright (c) 2003-2008 SIL International (http://www.sil.org/), with Reserved Font Names "Gentium" and "SIL".

Edited by Glenn S. Ritchey III.
Design and layout by AWG INC, operating as Glenn S. Ritchey III, under the directon of John Hoffman.
limb.fun / Instagram: @awginc

Sifting Press
Geneva, IL
Instagram: @siftingpress

For my daughter Grace—
May your beautiful existence forever
shine a light on this dark, despicable world.

"Description begins in the writer's imagination, but should finish in the reader's."

—Stephen King, *On Writing: A Memoir of the Craft*

INTRODUCTION

A young boy sits on a couch in his basement, shivering under a fleece blanket during the dead of winter. His friend from class sits up on the armchair two feet away. They are eagerly awaiting the start of the double-feature they planned as the final coming attractions preview comes to an end. The screen on the 27" television fades to black as the VHS inside the 1982 Panasonic VCR has only just begun to warm. The first film begins.

"New Line Cinema, Media Home Entertainment, Inc. & Smart Egg Pictures present" appears in white letters on the TV screen. A man in dirty black pants walks through a murky basement workshop; the young boys are immediately drawn to what plays out in the opening scene. At this moment, the man is sharpening a glove with razor-sharp knives at the end of each finger—both boys anticipate unsettling events to follow.

Later in the film, a half-naked teenage girl is flung about her bedroom by an invisible assailant; there are four slashes down her chest and dark red blood gushes from her wounds. Her gore spatters as she is dragged up the wall and onto the ceiling and then smeared all about the room. Both the boys look at each other and begin laughing; their laughter only intensifies as the scene progresses.

A few hours later, the boys are again hysterical with amusement during the second film, laughing uncontrollably as a possessed girl's head spins around in full circles without any seeming resistance. They find this scene even funnier than an earlier one where the girl used a crucifix to repeatedly stab herself in the crotch.

The second film has now ended and the boys are tired, but the adrenaline of forbidden joy will keep them up for another hour as they share crude jokes through attempts to suppress their laughter so as to avoid waking the adults upstairs.

"Those movies weren't even scary," the boy says.

"Nope, not bad at all," his friend replies.

As the one boy drifts off to sleep in the comfort of his basement, his friend lays awake a few feet away. He looks out the basement window, riddled with fear and anxiety. He shivers, not from the draft of the twelve-degree winter's air gliding across the tile floor, or from the fictional violence and horror in their viewings. His shivering stems from something else. He trembles at the thought of something hiding behind closed doors; his heart hurts at the idea of facing another moment of undisclosed trauma. He is, unbeknownst to his friend, afraid to go home the next morning.

For him, an evening of movies at a friend's place down the road is an escape from reality. It is twelve hours of solace—an inkling of proof that greener pastures exist. If only he could find a way to permanently surround himself with those movies in the company of his friend...

The movies were not even scary, he had concurred with his friend. For he is unfortunately aware, unbeknownst to his friend, that there are far scarier things out there.

***

Horror, terror, and fear are innately awful feelings one faces. I don't believe any person wakes up in the morning and hopes to experience fear. Coming from an American perspective, it seems our culture worships horror, terror, and fear for its entertainment value as it is tied to how we maintain a compulsion to consume. We endlessly seek opportunities to absorb those feelings through books, movies, television, and games, chasing after this genre and not letting it out of our sight. If there is content set to arrive, we make sure we're right there to greet it with open arms.

When I say "we," I strictly refer to the fans, of course. There are some who simply do not desire fright and do not partake in such terrifying gratification. Perhaps they just find no appeal in the sensation of fear. Regardless, to say that most cultures embrace horror as an entertainment genre would be an understatement. Ingesting such mental chaos is hardly abnormal, morbid or immoral to the average person nowadays. Such begs the potentially obvious question of why we, the fans of horror, gravitate towards the macabre for personal enjoyment—why do we enjoy this darkness so much?

Considering the nature of horror media as a pastime beyond my own experiences, I could answer the previous question by suggesting that we seek to understand and validate the inverse of happiness. The pursuit of joy perpetuates itself and reflects a craving that assumes more sympathy than other desires. People want to enjoy their lives; they generally don't want to be murdered, injured, stalked, or scared. But when reality approaches, these horrors have the potential to be as normal and accepted in life as anything positive. Danger tends to be afoot when least expected.

When faced with this daunting reality, it seems counterproductive to run, hide, or fight. Those actions tend to prolong fears, or even turn them into terrible risks. Instead, attempting to, or seeking to turn those fears into the same enjoyments sought in the positive, beautiful, simple and natural aspects of life more closely resembles the pursuit to turn pain into pleasure. Thus, when I consider horror as a form of entertainment with such potential to reflect existentialism, I realize my joy in watching movies where people get their heads chopped off, or in reading a story about an abandoned insane asylum, represents an ongoing attempt to self-manage my own fears.

By exposing ourselves to an imaginative depiction of exaggerated terror, we achieve a sense of freedom from our own uneasiness. We accept our fears in the real world by acknowledging them in a safer environment, one that cannot actually harm us in any way. Darryl Jones writes, "The classic argument in defense of the brutality of horror is the concept of catharsis—the act of witnessing artistic representations of cruelty, monstrosity, pity and fear purges the audience of these emotions, leaving them psychologically healthier."[1] Likewise, we tend not to ignore the evil potentially lurking in the next neighborhood over, in the run-down and isolated farmhouse, or along the forbidden path that we avoid when walking home—all of which are places where danger may claim inno-

---

1 Darryl Jones, *Horror: A Very Short Introduction* (New York: Oxford UP, 2021), 30.

cent victims who have no hope of escape. Instead, we indulge in an awful truth: despite the happiness we wish to find, the world can be a nasty, ugly and deceitful place. It can be a haven for those who we have come to realize are the true villains out there: not ghosts, but manipulators; not werewolves, but abusers; not vampires, but murderers; and all of the other real-life terrors that sometimes find us, even in our own homes.

There is much to fear from these literal demons that walk among us in this world and in our societies. Jones also states that "The very space occupied by the slasher—the suburban home—became uncanny by his presence: basements and bedrooms became labyrinths, and even in a modest home, no one could hear you scream."[2] At the end of the day, though, when I write this, I think that maybe real-life terror makes grabbing the pillow during the scary parts of a movie look less like worry or anxiety and more like a blissful form of pleasure. Maybe screaming in the middle of the theater as a victim onscreen meets their final second of life will help remind us that we are, in fact, safe in that moment. And maybe happiness is staying inside on a cold evening, curling up near a warm fire with a new horror story, and indulging in the menacing content across its pages—by all means, we deserve an escape from the dangers of reality whenever possible.

John Hoffman
March 2024

---

2 Jones, 110.

Solomon Trail was inspired by a story that I read as a kid called "The Walk," from Alvin Schwartz's Scary Stories To Tell In The Dark. The story details two men walking along a ghastly landscape, spotting each other and acknowledging their fear of one another as they continue toward their seemingly parallel destinations.

My story pulls from that uncomfortable, eerie atmosphere and indulges further in the common fear of being followed by a mysterious stranger. Such is, in my opinion, one of the most terrifying and ordinary things that can happen to a person. The difference between being followed and being murdered also interests me, for there are times when a sudden element of surprise is involved in the latter; a murderer wants you gone and takes care of it when the time comes.

But to involve one's prey in a game of cat-and-mouse, where they must continually escape those advances with the assailant's intentions widely uncertain, always disturbed me the most in books, movies, and even in those real-life news stories where victims were harassed rather than outright eliminated. There was far more malicious intent and pure sociopathy implied in any of the stalking cases I delved further into.

It got to the point where I felt the victims might have been better off dead over what they had been subjected to during their final moments; sometimes it could even last up to days of torment. These occurrences all seemed to elicit a more unique type of fear: The longer one tries to escape dictates how long one remains in a state of increasing panic.

SOLOMON TRAIL

Henkleman, Missouri was a town of many urban legends; hundreds of mysterious occurrences over centuries had graced the community. They were bizarre tales of uncertainty that kept young children up at night in their beds, and those same tales made for great adult conversation pretty much anywhere else. Some of them began being told as early as the 1600s, while others had sprouted up in more recent times. In a largely unincorporated hamlet of no more than 350 hopeless romantics of life, these stories didn't just keep people entertained; they kept them fascinated with their roots and loyal to their community. The stories were what kept that boring town of Henkleman interesting, and thus kept its natives intact.

Without said natives, that town would have dried out in 1908 when nearby Whitford, Brandon, and Granville opened economy-launching textile mills, printing presses, and Livingston Foods, the Midwest's most dominant bakery commodity and Granville's claim to fame. That's not to say those locals who were more ambitious didn't travel for work, but they stayed loyal enough to keep their population afloat. And anyway, everyone else settled at the neighborhood grocers and hardware stores or drank themselves slowly to death way out in the cornfields. Attribute it all to the aforementioned loyalty if you will—the Henkleman townies weren't going anywhere.

Yes, with a town as rich with lore as Henkleman, you could only bet on the stories being the glue that held the sub-society together; it was something to believe in. None of those urban legends, however, involved the old man on Solomon Trail. As fate would have it, that discovery was reserved for one boy, a teenager named Timothy Gates. And with every centuries-old tale of terror needing to establish its roots at some point in time, and somewhere in this forsaken world, there's always going to be someone who experiences it first.

Timothy, *Tim* to just a few friends, lived in 1972 Chitt, Missouri, a village so small and insignificant it made Henkleman look like a neighboring metropolis. But alas, when you live right on the border they're one and the same to you, and Timothy spent nearly every minute of his time outside his house in the larger town.

Timothy's father, Arthur Gates, was nearly sixty years old. He was a landscaper who was kept in business solely by laborers who had to work 55-hour weeks in Whitford or Granville. They were men who were inevitably too busy or too drunk after work to care for their own lawns, but they still just barely afforded to keep them looking as though they still could. Art Gates took on hours during the spring and summer—and just halfway past one month in the fall, too, if he was lucky—so that he would have just enough money to feed his son and his wife, Ann Gates. But during late November and most of December, there was a sheer non-existence of landscaping services, so, Art also worked and shivered in the cashier's shed from morning 'til late night at Franklin's Tree Farm. This annual pop-up Christmas tree outlet always stood right behind Roger's Supermarket in Downtown Henkleman. With that little bit of extra cash during the dead season, aging Art Gates managed to keep his family afloat while Ann spent her days lying in bed, terminally ill and suffering through a long and potentially final bout with breast cancer.

The hours were long, the weather was typically brutal, and the old man never saw his son during that brief period chasing backup income. He could scarcely care for his withering partner and he had nearly given up hope for her recovery at this point. It was no life to lead, and it was no different than most anyone else in the Henkleman area. It was a town of the struggling and the desperate with most trying their absolute best to succeed, but all of them were more or less numb to the pain.

It was mid-October and there were no more Henkleman lawns to attend to. So during the Autumn of '72's very last moments, Timothy had counted the days before his father would have to begin working the all-day and all-night shifts at Franklin's. Snow flurries appeared every nine or ten days; they foreshadowed the menacing winter to come but were no match for the treacherous Midwest winds that blasted them into obscurity. Thus, the tree business had not yet arrived with their annual load of pines, and Timothy found himself able to spend the most amount of time possible with Dad—just for a few weeks, before the old man would disappear for the next six.

It was a time they both looked forward to despite the halo of misfortune that hung over their home: a maternal presence that was weak and dying. The time had not yet come to grieve her absence. However, there was simultaneously no real possibility of quality time beyond keeping her company while she rested in pain. Timothy and Arthur had each other, and perhaps that buffer period in between paychecks was the time they needed to test their bond.

At fourteen years old, Timothy started his first year at Henkleman High back in late August, and for the first time, the school was not just down the road from the family shack on the outskirts of Chitt, as the elementary school for grades one through eight had been; Henkleman High was a six-mile hike. Arthur had been driving Timothy to and from the new school so he wouldn't need to walk so far, especially when it began to get cold out. This was not an issue throughout the landscaping job and during the short buffer period after business died, but before either of them knew it, November 25th arrived and the weeks of father and son time had come to an end. Arthur had to go back to work at Franklin's, and Timothy would need to get himself home from school until winter break.

For young Timothy that season, terror would come in two forms, and the irony of how they correlated would go on to become legendary. The first form was one that most teenage boys, and girls, even—possibly more so—tend to go through at some point during adolescence.

Now, there was nothing particularly unordinary about the boy from Chitt, at least not from the perspective of what differences tend toward utter torture amongst peers. Timothy had similar hobbies as any teenager. He was of average height, or rather, a few inches shy of it depending on who you put him up against—he was not overweight, or underweight; albeit he was skinny enough. He had no outrageous acne and was certainly in a better situation there than others in his age group. He was reasonably kempt, and there was nothing outright peculiar about his physicality.

Timothy was also shy, in what many would call a conventional sense, which undoubtedly could've been a contributing factor to bullies being naturally drawn to him. Still, by all means, Jake Lansing had the outright audacity to give Timothy any trouble. There was no justification for such treatment: ridicule, and taunting, which would then lead to threats and physical abuse. Alas, in the world of juvenility, justified or not, anything can just "be." But as a wise person once said, what goes around shalt turn the corner and come right back swinging.

Timothy's problems with Jake and his small crew of malefactors began during Henkleman High School basketball tryouts, which resulted in Timothy joining the JV team. They'd had their first practice in late October, just a few weeks before Timothy would become ride-less after school. Whether it was the wrong place at the wrong time or some type of omen for a further spectacle to come, Timothy found himself cornered in the locker room after they'd all hit the showers one afternoon.

"You've done a pretty good job of avoiding us, Gates," Jake said, kicking things off.

It was true, they had taunted poor Timothy with increasingly outlandish insults ever since they first spotted him on the court. They had refused to pass him the ball. They had laughed when he missed a shot. And Timothy's shyness had prevented him from giving them the time of day that they were looking to get out of him.

"What do you think, you're better than us or something?" one of Jake's pals echoed. "Who the hell are you?" he barked.

Timothy undressed quickly while staring at the floor. His hands trembled, making his fear apparent.

"Hey, eyes up, Freshman," Jake said, violently tapping Timothy on the left shoulder. Timothy made eye contact and spoke.

"I've got no problem with you, Jake; I don't even know you."

"That's what I thought. Next time I see you, we'll be better friends, eh?" And with that, he and his buddies turned and walked off, coldly laughing in the distance.

The second encounter with Jake was worse. It was a few weeks into November, only one day before Timothy would no longer have a ride home from school, when another one of Jake's followers tripped Timothy on his way back from taking a piss; it was after practice again, but Timothy fought back this time. He threw a weak punch that missed the sidekick's face and barely landed on his collarbone, causing virtually no damage. It was a strike, nonetheless.

"Oh, that's it!" Jake exclaimed, enthusiastically taking the lead and chasing Timothy back to his locker. A few shoves and a punch to the gut later, Timothy, still in his gym clothes, snatched his things and took off running toward the doors to the hallway. With his books and his street clothes clutched at his side, Timothy barely made it out through the massive double-door entrance with his attackers right on his tail.

Arthur Gates had been sitting at the wheel of the family Ford Country Squire, staring straight forward in a daze, his wife's condition cluttering his deteriorating mind. As his son ran up to the car, he barely noticed that the bullies chasing Timothy out to the parking lot quickly turned around and ran back into the school. But all Timothy could think about, after swiftly climbing into his father's car, was that no one would be waiting for him out front again until school started up after winter break.

Miraculously enough, Jake was absent the following day, and Timothy didn't have to endure any nonsense from anybody that afternoon. As most victims of bullying well know, no group of insecure followers function without a leader. During November 25th's basketball practice, and right after, Timothy didn't so much as receive a set of eyes from any of them, let alone a peep.

Leaving the school that day at 4:30 PM, Timothy decided to take a possible shortcut as he began his first attempt to make it home by himself. He had observed an alternate route while staring out the window on the drives to and from school with his father.

Solomon Trail was not much of a trail at all, despite its name on the Henkleman map; it was more of a long stretch of oak trees lining miles of farmland just above a raised hill. From what Timothy could piece together on those drives to school, the edge of the farmland split apart perpendicularly from Highway 32. There, he had seen the second of only two main roads leading them out of Chitt and to Henkleman High and it appeared to shoot straight back towards their house; it would be a long diagonal trip, regardless.

Walking just fifty feet down Highway 32, away from the school, Timothy veered off to begin following the stretch of trees instead of staying on the main roads. Just as he made his way across the street, the sun began to set.

The looming darkness combined with the bitter chill of a winter transition made Timothy uneasy from as early as the first half-mile. It was like a warning the world seemed to whisper assertively to young Timothy, telling him to turn back around and take a more familiar route.

Staring straight ahead, the isolated home Timothy approached was not even a speck in the distance. He was mostly positive he was headed in the right direction, but by the time his destination would become remotely visible, the grayness that was nearly pitch black had engulfed the atmosphere and all the landscapes were mere dark shadows escaping the moonlight. For the first five minutes of the journey, traffic from nearby Route 7 was still audible and the vehicle headlights of men and women coming home from work still shone through the early evening. But as Timothy continued further along his diagonal trek, no evidence of humanity or civilization, beyond farmland, was at all within sight.

The wind started to pick up and was seemingly coming from all directions; it was as if Timothy was trapped in some sort of personalized tornado. Leaves flew past him as the sound of treacherous rustling and violent cold air pierced his eardrums. At one point, Timothy wasn't even sure he was still following the line of oak trees anymore, fearing he had unwillingly wandered off into the middle of a vast field.

There was a sudden increased intensity of leaves rustling louder and more abrasive than the ones swirling on the ground in front of him. It steered Timothy back in the direction of the raised farmland he had attempted to scale. He recognized the sound of feet—possibly in boots—dredging through crumbling foliage, lazily unable to take proper steps but pushing on with an aggressive sense of urgency; someone was trailing behind him.

Timothy turned around and a gust of harsh dust and sharp debris attacked his squinted eyes like a hail storm. In the midst of the shadowed trees just a few feet above, he could just barely see the figure forcing its way through the forest. The figure's movement, blurry and scattered, perfectly correlated with the rustling noises as hoards of leaves were brushed aside with each daunting step.

A pang of regret flooded Timothy's heart as he turned to again face that uncertain path. Why couldn't he have just gone back the way he and his father initially came...

As he began to increase his speed, he pushed determinedly against the forceful winds that continued knocking him in all directions. The rustling continued to intensify and it was undeniable at this point that a human was following Timothy. He briefly wondered if it was Jake Lansing. No, it couldn't be. Something far more nightmarish was afoot. Something stranger, more unprecedented. Jake would've had others with him, anyway. Whoever was tailing Timothy Gates in these terrifying moments was likely a lone human, but whoever they were could not possibly be someone he would have known.

After what seemed like forever, and yet like no time at all, of desperately sprinting away from this mystery stalker, a horizon of homes ever so slightly illuminated by street lights appeared in the distance. It was the first neighborhood of Henkleman just over the Chitt border. Timothy knew he was within a mile of home.

Behind him, the strip of forest was as dark as it had been, and this malevolent force of horror continued to follow. Although Timothy had become winded long beforehand, he just now started to lose speed, and it was this drop in momentum that allowed him to notice his chaser slowing down with him. Whoever this happened to be, they intended to follow Timothy closely rather than catch up with him; they were toying with him. Timothy was drenched from his forehead to his ankles in a numbingly freezing layer of sweat, yet he pushed on. His sides ached such dreadful pains that he couldn't help but cry out every few seconds. At last, he started to come up on a street outlining the nearing neighborhood. Coming to his senses too little and too late, he began to wonder why he continued to overexert himself, knowing this harasser hadn't yet exploited his exhaustion. Timothy turned back around, still pulsating with terror, and gave his legs a slight break while keeping his guard up. The street lamps provided significantly more light and, for a split second, it did not appear to Timothy that he was being followed any longer.

The trees had ended about thirty feet back; he had potentially made it to safety. But the stalker emerged from the very last of the oak trees, matching Timothy's diminishing pace, and stopped shortly after. He now stared straight ahead at Timothy from mere yards away.

A man covered in an oversized dark brown cloak appeared elderly and frail, yet by no means was he thin or emaciated. Hunched over, his complexion was somewhere between ghostly and lifeless; a stringy, pale gray beard nearly covered his entire face, making it difficult to point out any distinct features. Still, even from across the plain preceding the street, Timothy noticed dark circles and droopy bags under his eyes. As if the terror was unable to end with their chase coming to a halt, those eyes were also filled with a cruel madness; each second his gaze persisted was

9

a menacing threat. Timothy shuddered in his presence while still fighting to catch his breath from the debilitating sprint.

"What do you want?!" Timothy pleaded for some type of clarity as to why this spine-chilling occurrence had plagued his evening.

The man said nothing, but began to slowly inch forward; his heavy, rubber boots dragged as he took small steps across frosted blades of grass. Timothy's knees buckled, but his feet stayed firmly planted and he remained frozen stiff in his stance across the field; the poor boy was unable to bring himself to turn around and escape.

Failing to glisten in the combination of moonlight and streetlamp due to layers of jagged rust, the old man's blade made its first appearance. That blade clung tight to his right hand as if it had no handle—as if it were merely an extension of his palm—barely distinguishing itself against its owner's murky brown silhouette. Timothy no longer sensed danger; he now anticipated his end.

A few feet away now, his image crystal clear under the illuminating light above, the old man's arm ventured upward. Rising high into the air with the momentum of a roller coaster just about to make its drop, the ascending position of the rusty machete paused momentarily. Preserved in place and unable to look away, Timothy made direct eye contact with two pale blue eyes, as ice-cold and dead as the pending winter. Those eyes stared into his with zero emotion, rather they stared with an intent to destroy out of sheer instinct. The being before him appeared only as alive as the deceitful winds in the atmosphere.

Its arm began to come down swiftly as Timothy's eyes closed in one final instance of survival. The blade made a sickening, yet relieving crunch as it pierced a deep wedge into the brittle soil, less than three inches from Timothy's left foot. In the wake of several skipped heartbeats, Timothy allowed his eyes to peer open slowly, revealing that he had not been struck.

This is a dream. This isn't real.

Most unbelievable moments in life usually result in a shred of doubt, as if this couldn't be reality, and it takes a second to come to the ultimate realization: This *is* real. This *is* life.

Timothy came to his senses in disbelief and faced who he had initially known to be his predator. The creature continued to stare back, though its icy-blue eyes that were death itself moments earlier had now dissolved into a regular dark shade of brown; the demonic, ghostly image that had advanced toward Timothy now appeared to be human once more.

With his right hand still firmly clutching the blade that was submerged into the ground, he began to lift his alternate hand, slowly, but steadily, and he gestured with his left index finger in a way that nearly grazed Timothy's right cheekbone. The boy panted in fear as the old man extended his finger behind him.

"Go," he whispered at Timothy, in a ghastly echo as ambient as the horrific landscape among them.

After piercing silence, the command was repeated, "*Go,*" in the same formidable hush. Timothy was being summoned home.

Regaining all his vitality that once was, Timothy turned and ran towards his neighborhood, never once looking back to see if he was being followed yet again. By the time he reached the solace of his shack just past the border of Henkleman and Chitt, there was no one else in plain sight.

Somewhere, somehow, the old man had decided to spare young Timothy.

***

That was the first time Timothy took Solomon Trail home. By no means did he intend to repeat that journey, not after the terror he experienced.

It was the following morning, and Timothy had settled into a chair at the breakfast table while his father was just starting to make coffee.

"How was your walk home, son?" Arthur Gates asked after greeting him.

There was a brief pause. Timothy failed to utter a response before his father continued, "Little chilly yesterday, eh? Gonna get even colder this week, I'm afraid. You look like you didn't get much sleep."

It was true, he hadn't.

"It was fine, Dad," Timothy replied to his father, who was slaving over the Mr. Coffee like his life depended on a fresh pot. "I just had a little insomnia last night. Some coffee would be great, though."

"You're drinking coffee now? Christ, where does the time go?" he said with a warm smile and an old-aged chuckle.

Most everything about his father lightened any type of mood, if nothing else than the mere twinkle in his eye when he spoke to you, and in that moment, Timothy couldn't help but perk up. But there was not a chance he would mention the truth about his commute. His father had enough on his mind with the job, not to mention his wife having had her own trouble sleeping that previous night. Timothy could always sense the guilt and shame his dad felt about not being able to pick his son up from school in the first place.

"And how was Franklin's, Dad?"

"Ah, jeez." He paused, pouring a cup of straight black coffee, no cream, no sugar. "Well, let's just say it's going to be a long season, Timmy."

Timothy knew that was true. But while he desperately tried to wash away the previous evening's chilling encounter from his mind with no luck at all, he knew he still had a bigger problem on the horizon. And besides, there was no chance he'd ever take that same way home again.

***

Like God's cruel and simple way of positioning fate just to tantalize a person with anxiety, Jake Lansing was the first person Timothy made eye contact with after walking through the double doors of Henkleman High. He had hoped his new nemesis would still be absent for whatever reason he had been the day prior, but there was no such luck.

Amazingly, Jake didn't budge from the huddle he was in with a few of his cronies, and he seemingly didn't even stop his conversation to point Timothy out to the others. But he did offer the slightest of smirks, his eyes squinting just enough to mock and condescend Timothy's existence from all the way across the main hallway. When one person looks at another the way Jake did Timothy, there are no words needed. The disrespect was crystal clear, and that patronizing leer of Jake's foreshadowed an unpleasant afternoon; an altercation between the two of them was imminent.

Anxiously and with a deadening pit in his stomach, Timothy walked past the group and disappeared into the sea of students making their way to the first class of the day.

During the next few hours, Timothy thought back to the previous evening—his chase, and the reality that no harm had technically been done to him. The image of the spectral old man that had callously followed him home would not leave his mind, and simultaneously, he had wondered why he had been put through such anguish. Had the old man initially intended to hack him to bits with his machete before suddenly changing his mind? Was there a purpose to any of it? Or was it all just a feeble attempt to scare a young teenage boy who carelessly chose the wrong route...was it perhaps a domanial warning, a declaration of territory...

The fact that Timothy was now safe produced a relieving sensation that there was possibly nothing to fear. A decision had been made by the man to let him go free. He had been lucky in this sense, so long as he could continue to avoid those parts of Henkleman and remain safe—was there much else to ponder?

This feeling didn't remain, and fear crept back in as Timothy's fickle thought process continued to consume and distract him throughout the day. Here and there, the constant reminder of basketball practice that afternoon would further make his stomach feel sicker than the common flu ever had.

The practice itself was surprisingly absent of torture. The boys left him fully alone during the warm-up, then during the five-on-five scrimmage, and then during the walk back to the locker room. The same way the rest of Jake's crew had virtually ignored him a day earlier, they, along with their big chief, followed the same protocol; Timothy had wondered if maybe they had grown bored of him. He had bravely attempted to stand his ground the week prior, after all, refusing to back down albeit still showing a bit of fear and eventually running. But maybe that shred of resistance had effectively killed their momentum. It wouldn't be unheard of...

Timothy looked around the locker room after getting dressed. The silence, except for a mere shower still echoing way back in the distance, provided reassurance that perhaps this would be a day free of problems. There was no sign of Jake or any of his friends nearby.

To play it just a little safer, Timothy waited around for another ten minutes. If anyone was out there scheming in the hallway, they'd either come in to find him or call it a day and leave. Hoping for the latter, Timothy patiently counted the minutes before he decided it was time to head home.

Pushing through the exit doors to the parking lot at the entrance of the school, Timothy stepped outside and glanced at his watch; it was 4:47 PM. The sun had already begun its descent and was nearly halfway set.

Walking towards the dimly lit Highway 32, which led to the main road back to Chitt, Timothy saw a group of boys standing together at the edge of the parking lot. He froze, still unsure of exactly who they were, but anticipating they were exactly who he feared they might be.

"What took you so long, Gates?!" Jake's enthusiastic voice threatened across the wind.

Timothy knew that when facing an adversary, one always has to choose between conflict or avoidance. At this moment, he hadn't yet convinced himself to turn around and run back into the school. He stood still, contemplating the option to face them head-on. Jake, with a few cronies right behind him, took the liberty to swiftly walk towards him through the parking lot.

"Making us all wait to give you a pounding, eh?" Jake said, with the sound of a few barely audible cackles in the background, "Glad you could make it."

It's going to be worse this time. They waited until I was outside of the building. They planned this.

There was no way to run past them if he intended to still follow the main roads. Even if he could outrun them, they were fully blocking his path. An inevitable decision was right in front of Timothy now, taunting him, mocking him.

Where else can you go, Timmy? What are you gonna do, hide back in the school like the wimp they think you are?

He knew in his head that it was crazy, even while in panic mode, but a part of him imagined that he could somehow lose them by taking the forbidden shortcut, or, perhaps their interest in the chase would wane as he faded into the darkness of the trees.

The darkness of the trees...

Where else can you go, Timmy?

As Jake advanced towards him, less than twenty feet away, Timothy turned right and took off running. At that moment, fear had left his body and a sense of daring nerve took over his psyche, catapulting him vehemently in the direction of Solomon Trail.

Jake and the others followed, sprinting meager yards behind their prey. Timothy had gotten a slight head start and could run reasonably fast in comparison, but the crew began slowly inching their way closer and closer, chipping away at his lead.

The impending darkness loomed as Timothy attempted to run harder and faster, utilizing his memory of the previous evening to stay on track and scale the endless line of oak trees. After minutes that seemed more like hours of frantic dashing past tree after tree, the sun had completely set, and Timothy could feel his chest burning as his adrenaline began to fail him. Whichever way he had managed to outrun his tormenter the night before had become an unknown blip in history, and Timothy was just about ready to run out of fuel. Still, he pushed himself to keep racing forward, moaning in pain out into the vastness of the field ahead.

In the midst of the pitch blackness surrounding the entire landscape, the vaguely familiar and intense sound of increased rustling began. Leaves crunched in the distance, and Timothy could hear those same boots dredging through rocks and frozen clumps of soil. Simultaneously, Jake had picked up his pace and was right on his tail now.

He's going to get me this time.

With a thud and a stabbing flash of pain, Timothy felt his back struck by a violent shove of two hands directly behind him. He tripped due to the force and tumbled down onto the hardened mixture of dirt and grass below.

Jake stood over him, slightly out of breath but mad with triumph. "Nice try, buddy," he said, panting.

With a kick to the ribs followed by the snickering laughter of everybody else that surrounded the two of them, Jake unloaded on poor Timothy, serving him the beginning blow of what was sure to be a ruthless beating. But through the sharp agony in his side and the sounds of apathy towering over him, Timothy could still make out the baleful sound of leaves rustling around the trees—louder now, and closer.

Jake leaned down with his left hand and seized Timothy by the collar of his winter jacket. He pulled Timothy slightly upwards and sneered at him, face to face.

Louder and louder. Closer and closer...

"Every time you run, it'll be worse," said Jake, the minty breath from his chewing gum invading Timothy's nostrils, "this is nothing."

Closer...

Jake raised his right arm and balled up his fist. As he was about to bring down the second of harsh blows, his left-hand grip on Timothy's collar loosened in an instant. Jake jolted backward as Timothy fell a few inches back down to the ground.

Barely visible and only a mirage of dark moving shadows, Timothy saw something rapidly swinging through the dead air, unsure of who was who. All he could make out was a crowd of bodies going berserk and a slew of panicked yells enhancing the chaos.

Several of the crowd that had chased him, possibly all of them with Jake included, were running in the opposite direction, and some of them were screaming. Timothy could not tell who, if anyone at all, was still there with him after the crowd dispersed. All he knew was that a dark silhouette, resembling who could be none other than the old man, stood still above him.

Whatever had just occurred had happened very quickly, and Timothy, still lying on his back, had barely had a chance to move. Upon realization that he was no longer being attacked, he scooted himself back a few feet and quickly scrambled to his feet.

The same figure he had encountered the night before now stood three yards away. After staring through the darkness and allowing his eyes to slightly adjust, Timothy could see the old man's face staring back, directly at him. The eyes belonging to that ghostly face shimmered with a pale blue fury, once again suggesting a presence more feral than civilized. And, just as the creature had done during their first encounter, it raised its right arm to point in the direction back towards Timothy's neighborhood. Before it spoke, those rage-filled eyes reverted to a less threatening, human-like shade of brown once more.

"Go," he whispered in that same creepy murmur.

The resonance in his voice was less apparent this time; it was as if it were dying out. There was not an ounce of light nearby, not even from the traffic about a mile west of them. Struggling to view anything in the pitch black, Timothy slowly backed away from the inconspicuous figure repelling him and turned around. Exhausted and still struggling to catch his breath, he began to sluggishly walk in the direction of home.

***

For the second night in a row, Timothy experienced zero sleep. Feelings of uneasiness and confusion flooded his brain, like a series of film reels that had been mixed up and played at the wrong speed.

He no longer feared whomever, or *whatever*, had been following him. He knew he had been saved that second evening, in addition to being spared from God-only-knows-whatever fate he had tempted during the first encounter. Two opportunities to do away with young Timothy had resulted in negligence on the count of the old man on Solomon Trail. By all means, Timothy was lucky to be alive. But was he ever really in danger?

The mystery of this unknown creature that only seemed to come out on that one stretch of land was overwhelming to the point that Timothy needed to forget about it to save his sanity. At one point, maybe it would all seem like a scary dream, or akin to the many urban legends that graced the conversations of local townsfolk. Timothy still made no mention of it to his father.

Several police cars, an ambulance, and a fire truck were parked on Highway 32, lights flashing and all, when Arthur Gates pulled the family Ford up to the front entrance of the school that morning.

"I wonder what happened," Timothy's father said to him.

"I don't know," Timothy replied. And he wasn't lying, at least not completely. The part he omitted was that he was sure it had something to do with whatever had happened the night before. And instantly, a sickening feeling, fully familiar by now, wrenched Timothy's gut and produced an unbearable amount of anxiety-ridden pain.

News of a murdered teenage boy made its way around the school at around 11:00 AM through faculty-led meetings in each classroom. It wasn't until after lunch, closer to 1:00 PM, that the victim was announced to be a student at Henkleman High, identified as one Jacob Lansing, with three additional students being taken in for questioning. Jake's body, along with his severed head, was found in the middle of the field adjacent to the school, just about a half-mile down Solomon Trail.

After hearing about the other students who were to be brought in, all of whom had taken turns mocking him that season, Timothy wondered if his time would come for questioning as well. Would Jake's band of loyal followers name him as an additional witness? Would they name him as *the* suspect? Would they even admit why they had all been in that field the previous night?

That day, school was canceled for the rest of the week, and all students were sent home early. As Timothy approached the exit doors to the front entrance, he could already see the cars lined up to pick up the other students. He imagined the feeling of relief that would accompany each of their homes that day, the lucky feeling the parents must have had knowing that their children were safe, *alive*, and had not suffered like unlucky Jacob Lansing.

At that moment, Timothy stepped through the double doors out to the parking lot and smiled to himself as he experienced an ever-so-slight inkling of peace for the first time that week. He began walking towards Highway 32 and turned the corner to follow the main roads back home.

I often sit and think about the paths we all take in life. Some of them are by choice, while others are laid out for us in early childhood, or even from birth. If one were to believe in fate, then the cards we're dealt in life are completely random; we cannot control the hand. One person may flourish in delight, while another may fight an excruciating, uphill battle. "Life's not fair," is what is often said to rationalize this imbalance.

Our cards shape our personalities and lives. While we can alter the paths we're on, what if the factors that shaped those paths retroactively changed without us knowing? What would that transition be like as it plays out in the present?

Madness would ensue, I'd think.

OIL SPILL

"Metal—"

The dimly lit room glistened. Everywhere he looked, it was all he could see.

"—like a metallic shine, a puddle of metal."

The line between reality and imagination had blurred past recognition. This entire experience was driving him mad.

"Your face..."

Dr. Cohart looked puzzled; he was uncomfortable. His calm and collected expression had distorted into a sideways frown, and Sean could no longer tell if it was real or just an illusion that matched the sparkle of everything in front of him; everything was becoming engulfed in that shining metallic substance. It was so threatening that it made him feel fear and severe pain; the pain urged him to fight back against whatever was going to attack him...

"What do you mean 'my face,' Sean?"

"It's gray, it's made of metal. It shines like metal, at least, like the puddle—the oil spill, or whatever it was. This all began when I saw it. And it's *all* I can see now. It's even on you now, on your desk, the bookshelf—"

"Close your eyes, Sean," Cohart said, his delivery carrying the slightest hint of impatience and frustration peppering his tone. This session was

21

welding Cohart into unprofessionalism; Sean could feel it. He laid back, resting his head on the cool and firm tail end of the light gray chaise in his psychologist's office. As his eyes closed, the glistening of the metallic substance dissolved with what light there was in the room.

This is in my head, there is no metallic shine. It's all in my head; it's just my mind playing tricks on me when I open my eyes. It's not real.

But then the memories flooded in. It was like his mind was a dam and these memories were bursting it open, smashing the barrier apart to lend passage to waves of trauma. When the glistening stopped, in poured those memories, those images—the reminiscence of brutality. Every fucking time...

That tantalizing imagery was not exclusive to eyes wide shut. It all came and went as it pleased, like real memories do; but these memories never existed before that day in the parking lot of The Pound.

"Now it's just pain; it's just violence."

"What do you mean, Sean?" the doctor asked. "What is pain? What is violence?"

"I can't do it anymore, doc," Sean said, forcing the quiet in his delivery. It was all he could do to keep from crying out, from having an episode, despite how many were already circling in his head. They were already happening. They didn't need to happen on the outside. But did it matter?

"There's just too much. I never did these things."

Dr. Cohart stuttered, "These memories, Sean—" looking at the teenager lying down in front of him. While it was more than clear his patient was frantic, there was a calmness about him. A desperate calmness, a resistance to react. In that moment, and many prior, Cohart truly felt for the boy. But he also did not know what to suggest to him, as rare of a circumstance as that was in his profession. "—you say they aren't real?"

"I never experienced these things," Sean said, shivering all of a sudden from what felt like the coldest of drafts. "But I did. I know they're real, because I can feel that they are."

✦✦✦

"I haven't felt like this in a long time," she said. "Thank you, Sean...really."

He stared into her pale green eyes as she gently rested her hand on his, slowly drizzling her fingertips across the hair on his knuckles. The way she gazed back at him was pure. She was appreciative of his kindness. She cared about him; she was infatuated with him.

What a beautiful girl, what a wonderful person—she deserves every moment of it.

But, he wondered what kind of sadness or void hid behind her appreciation. What was missing, why hadn't she felt like this in a long time? Was her life riddled with pain, had her previous relationship gone sour? Or maybe she had just been so busy with nursing school that life had become consumed with responsibility and its stresses—without a break, without any chance to enjoy a nice dinner in a handsome young man's apartment...

"Don't mention it," he replied, breaking eye contact and shifting his focus to the floor.

"Is everything alright? You seem...troubled."

"Nope, everything is fine, I might have had just a little too much wine," he said, chuckling. "I don't normally drink much."

"Well, this has been a lovely date. I might be falling for you already..." She let out a giggle and leaned back onto the nearest arm of Sean's couch.

The confidence of this girl—her openness. She is comfortable. She wants to be here. She appreciates everything about this. She is allowing herself to enjoy it.

And it's almost time...

They'd met outside of the New York Public Library on 125th Street when they happened to hail the same cab. From the moment Sean laid eyes on this beauty, he was captivated. There was a bit of everything about her: an elegance, a shyness, an eager adventurousness about her, a goofiness, an arrogance, even an intensity, possibly a dark one, that seemingly hid in the shadows of her blatant kindness and gentleness. All of this was seen immediately through those pale blue eyes—like an open invitation to gaze through the window of her soul. Girls like this were the largest of mysteries, the most intriguing—the ones with a story to tell that, no matter what it contained, you wanted to know and be a part of. Sean did; he wanted in.

"Are you going to take it from me?" she had abruptly asked, in a way that was both playful and taunting.

"I just might," he replied, wielding zero shame in his flirtatious wit, "or we could share the ride, perhaps?"

"Perhaps our next destination could be the same?" she added, playing along as if it were a rehearsed line, "Why make the driver go all over the city?"

"He'd be making double the fare. That wouldn't be right..."

She laughed and put her hand on his shoulder, giving him a light shove, smiling while staring into his eyes. An invitation. This was it; something was starting.

As it turned out, neither of them could devote the afternoon to each other, and that driver wound up cashing in on two different fares after all. She went to her book club meeting and he went to meet up with a friend who he had promised lunch. But neither left without exchanging numbers and making potential plans for an evening together that same week, whichever one ended up working for both of them. From there, it would be up to one of them to make the next move. Unsurprising to him, it was her. And as tradition might have it, she felt obligated to reach out after not hearing from him for a few days after that first night.

"I figured you'd have called by now," she said, hiding her desperation with playfulness.

"Ah, well," Sean said, "all that matters is we're talking now, right?" It was a smooth reply, free of accountability, but not without an underlying compliment attesting to his joy. "It's great to hear from you," he said.

And so the first date came quickly. That same night of the phone call, the pair decided to meet at Sean's apartment around 7:00 PM—her idea of a casual opening chapter to their burgeoning, and already potentially lustful, relationship. She offered to take a cab there. He said he would love to make her dinner and watch a movie together.

The forwardness of her offer, the shameless self-invitation into his private world almost fit her inevitable conclusion too well. Most ironically, it inspired Sean with a sense of guilt that directly conflicted with his unstoppable urge to—

But it was her immediate desire to be with him that counted the most. This was right; it was acceptable. Sean humbly but enthusiastically complied with her request and, with that, the stage was set.

So as it neared 10:00 PM on the night of the first date, after dinner and some passionate, yet reserved, light cuddling during the movie, she confessed that she was falling for him. Already, on night one.

"Do you mind if I use your bathroom?" she said next, allowing her previous statement to swirl around Sean's thoughts for a few minutes. She pressed her fingertips more firmly onto the top of his hand as she dragged them slowly away.

This fucking bitch must pay.

"Of course, it's right down that hall to the left," he said.

She crawled out from underneath his arms, wiggling her tiny waist as she stood up. Her light perfume smelled like roses, just enough to capture the essence of a girl who spent a good amount of time grooming herself for a possible night of sex—yet without the overpowering scent of someone who was trying just a bit too hard to seduce. It was a modest balance, and it was a perfect one.

As she walked away, she subtly shifted her hips from side to side, her tight black jeans rumpling with each movement. A cute blue flannel rested comfortably on her slender, but fit, upper half. Long, mousy brown hair, brushed to perfection, hung glamorously, down past her shoulders.

She has a fantastic body, and she really wants me to see it now.

And now was the time, the perfect moment. The bathroom door shut behind her, and up from the couch rose Sean, beginning to slowly tip-toe down the hall.

As he made his way, he grabbed a crewneck sweatshirt draped over an armchair. Sean waited patiently outside the bathroom door. He flicked a light switch, illuminating the hallway his new partner had just ventured in pitch blackness.

It was about a minute later that Sean heard the toilet flush, followed by some light humming, and then about forty seconds of silence.

She is admiring herself in the mirror, making sure she looks and smells as nice as she did when she last saw me.

***

Before another second seemed to pass, it appeared to Sean that her breath had stopped. Her eyes bugged out of her skull, an expression of shock and fear now permanently glued to her face like a mask—her *death mask*. In a flash, Sean found himself moments into the future; the buildup to this madness was merely a faint memory in his subconscious.

Eventually, and with clarity, Sean would recall her opening the bathroom door, how she quietly stepped out into the hallway, and immediately gasped a sound of pure joy at the sight of him standing before her.

"Oh!" he would remember her yelping, "You scared me." She'd then say with a playful sneer, as if she thought she knew exactly what Sean had in mind, "And what do you think you're doing over here, Mister?"

Bitch must pay...

He'd remember her starting to press her body up against his, leaning her face in for a soft, gentle, passionate kiss. He'd remember her beginning to throw her arms around him when he abruptly raised his arms up and out of her grasp, clinging tightly to the sweatshirt in his hands.

He'd see the image of her abruptly startled for the second time, more confused now, as he clutched both sleeves of the sweatshirt and aggressively brought both hands to her neck—a thick cotton barrier between her skin and his.

He'd recollect the immediate look of panic and fear in her eyes before contact was made, barely able to let out the slightest of shrieks before any sound she could make was rendered impossible due to her now crushed windpipe.

He'd revisit feeling his strength, madness, and rage kick into high gear, immediately, as he decided to squeeze as hard as possible from both sides, with the force of his grip focused not only on closing in on the skin around her trachea but on pushing her forward to begin slamming her head against the wall at the end of the hallway.

He'd remember clenching his teeth in impatient fury at the sight of her eyes shutting and opening again upon impact, realizing the blow to the back of her skull did not knock her out completely.

He'd replay the only sound coming from her mouth: a gagging noise, a crackling, scratchy croak that cut in and out as oxygen neither entered nor carbon dioxide exited her lungs.

But in the immediate present, that final moment of Carly's life might as well have dissipated into a non-existent past now that she was lifeless, lying in front of him with no more force needed to secure her. Her body became increasingly limp, and far more heavy as he slowly laid her down on the floor. All Sean could wonder at the time was how he had done such a thing. And simultaneously, a callous feeling of triumph, of pride...

Sean loosened his grip and lifted his hands away from her neck, pulling the sweatshirt away. Despite the torment he inflicted on the inside of her throat, there would be no way for anyone else to determine whose hands were responsible.

***

"And that was it. That was what happened."

"Sean—"

"No, no, no, it *didn't* happen. I didn't hurt her. I didn't kill her."

"Sean, if you are admitting to me you are a danger to—"

"Doc, I told you already."

Cohart's voice trembled along with his fingers, nearly dropping his pen to the floor. "Right, this is a memory," he said, in an uneasier tone than he had ever recognized from himself. He continued, "a memory you...have, but don't have."

"Right."

"Sean, you've never lived in New York City. Have you?"

"No."

"You still live with your parents," Dr. Cohart continued, "this memory of yours—it doesn't sound like you."

"I'm older in it, for sure. I've got a different life, I'm on my own. I'm meeting women in the city."

Sean paused, and he knew it had gotten to *that* point. Whether or not Cohart was here to help, he no longer believed a word of what he was hearing—no one would. Not one word anymore.

"I'm going insane, doc. I can feel that I did these things, but—"

"Let's go back to when this started, when you started to experience these indications of an 'alternate reality.' I want you to try and remember the day before. The day before the parking lot—I want you to try and remember what that was like. Where your life was—"

"I'm not even me anymore," Sean said, the calmness in his tone still there. Whether it was forced or natural, Cohart could no longer tell.

"Sean, please just try—"

"DR..."

"...COHART..."

A long silence deadened the dry, stale atmosphere in the tiny office. Cohart recognized that, at this moment, not only did he need time to collect his thoughts and carefully plan his next words but his patient should be given some space.

***

He hid and listened.

Did they think he couldn't hear them? He always wondered about that. Even at eight years old, Sean pondered whether there was a difference between exposure as outright disrespect or if it could just be accidental in these scenarios. Did they have such little regard for him that they could scream their heads off until their throats went sore, with no concern for his fear or sadness ... or were they too stupid, too distracted and caught up in their world, to notice that he was nearby and taking it all in?

The boy wondered as he listened to his father tearing Denise apart; the things his father said were things he was told not to say in school. The words his father used were words that meant bad things.

Whore.

Fucking whore.

Well, there'd be no chance he could ever say that in school. Even to Amy Hansworth, who no one liked anyway; he couldn't call her that.

Bitch.

Stupid fucking bitch.

But of course not, no way. Though he had heard Danny and Kyle say it about Mrs. Bradley before...

He also heard his father say those words to Denise many times, and he was hearing his father say them to Denise now, as Sean cradled his knees in the corner of his closet. The smell of old, rotting carpet and dust crept into his nose and throat as he breathed, heavily and slowly.

When is this going to end...

He listened carefully as they continued.

You're a fucking asshole. Who the fuck do you think you are...

Those words came from Denise this time; they were followed by the sound of broken glass and then the slamming of pantry doors, three in a row. The loud noises were more frightening than the words; there had been time to get used to the words. He had even heard some of those words yelled in his own face before. The noises, though familiar in their own way by now, never got old. In the house, any loud and abrasive sound that didn't come directly from the mouths of adults was the biggest cause for alarm. It meant things were getting bad.

There were leftovers from previous nights all throughout the downstairs portion of the house, where they fought most often. A new hole in the wall and maybe some shattered glass swept aside in the kitchen somewhere. A dented picture frame, no longer hanging, but stuck in between the couch and the living room wall.

Then there was what would have been an otherwise unusual sight: the tooth that was resting too comfortably on the floorboards by the radiator. Surrounding it were chunks of dirt and triangular pieces of broken ceramic. A dead, rotting ficus collapsed near the wreckage with no memory of better days. But the tooth, and the dark brown stain of dried blood spattered in a circle around it...

He knew where Denise had stood at the time, and he knew what his father had done.

He referred to these leftovers as his *reminders*. There was never silence in the home. The brutality may have died down at any given moment, but it was never gone. As he climbed the stairs to his room; as he opened the refrigerator door; as he turned on the TV; and as he wiped his shoes on the mat by the front door, nothing changed the fact that those walls closed in on him. Everything within those walls was real and those reminders were there to keep reality visible.

The sounds kept them alive.

The sounds were the worst part. But what reminders would be waiting for him the next morning when he crept down the stairs to go to school...

...what was waiting?

It wasn't over yet. This was a long one, and it was worse than usual. The doors slammed harder, and there was more broken glass.

I'm leaving. Have a nice fucking life.

Footsteps. Stomping across the living room, towards the front door. Followed by...

A louder stomping. Bigger footsteps. Those of a man. His father.

The sound of a two-second chase, followed by a slam, and then a scream: Denise's scream.

You stupid fucking bitch!

A second scream, a cry, an agonizing, defeating wail of pain and sacrifice.

Please. Please just—

Silence. Silence for a full minute. Followed by a thud, the loudest Sean ever heard. Even at eight years old, he knew what sound that was. Nothing else could produce a thud so loud—nothing other than a 128-pound body against a hardwood floor.

There!! What do you think?! Bitch, what do you think of that?! You didn't think you'd fucking pay now, DID YOU?!

Well, now you've fucking paid!!

His father.

***

It had been a few minutes.

A few minutes of dreadful silence that was awkward for Cohart. But to Sean, the silence was an unwanted break that allowed the demons to come creeping in like the intruders they were. And they brought brutality with them every time.

"My dad..."

More silence.

"I'm sorry, what did you say, Sean?"

Cohart had given him some time after the outburst. Sean's statements had not been consistent with one another, as if they were from different timelines. Nothing was making sense anymore.

"Nothing," Sean said, more quietly than ever.

He wasn't really sure who his dad was anymore. There was the father he knew he grew up with. The man who he played catch with in the backyard—the man who bought him a guitar for his eleventh birthday. That man.

A man who was happily married to his mother—not a man dating a woman named Denise, whom he clearly despised.

The positive memories were fading; new memories kept coming. And while Sean knew they were so unfamiliar and so intrusive, they felt like the truth. They felt like what really happened.

He flashed back to that night, the night his abusive, booze-fueled father had outdone himself. After hearing Denise's body hit the ground, Sean slowly and cautiously turned the knob of his closet door. It creaked with every quarter-turn; the creak was a harsh and threatening shriek of resistance that made his already rapid heart rate increase.

Once he had crept out of his room, down the hall, and carefully to the top of the stairs—so his father would not know he was awake—he leered

31

around the corner and saw her body. Denise was face down, and if she were on her back, the splotches of crimson splattered across her white t-shirt would have been all the more apparent. As Sean examined her corpse from afar, he saw more stab wounds decorating the tight black jeans that clung to her lifeless thighs; they were harder to make out but noticeably glistening in the moonlight that shone through the front window. There was blood all over her body, and four times that amount had formed a sickening pool on the floor around her.

The gruesome image before him was scored by the sound of the kitchen sink water splashing against his father's hands, apathetically mixed with the radio playing the Steve Miller Band classic "Abracadabra." That combination of sounds told an entirely separate story, one of a man who lacked remorse for his actions. Or maybe it told of a man who didn't know what to do with himself after those actions, desperately looking for a distraction from reality. But Sean had grown up with the former; it was the only version of the story he could trust.

The body was gone by morning. Sean crept down those stairs to go to school, trembling after a night without one second of sleep or even the slightest bit of rest. Before walking out the door to catch the bus, he looked back to see his father standing in the kitchen archway, staring forward with his eyes glowing red like a madman.

In that instant, Sean realized it had only been three and a half hours since the murder. On any other morning, he would have walked downstairs to his father snoring on the couch with his fingers still clutching a bottle of Jim Beam. This morning, his father had likely finished cleaning up his mess not more than a half-hour earlier.

"What are you looking at? Get out the door." There was so much hate, so much disdain in his callous demands.

Sean gulped a dry clump of air that tore up his throat on the way down. He didn't know what was causing his urge to speak up, but it was about to come out like vomit.

"Where's Denise, Dad?"

Without a second thought, his father took swift strides toward him, his boots alternating in stomps on the floorboards that shook the house like an earthquake. Before Sean could process the effect of his words, his father had lunged forward and struck him, knocking him right to the ground.

Sean was face down in the same spot he had found Denise only hours earlier, and the putrid stench of death still wafted from the floorboards. His father demanded, "I don't ever want to hear that bitch's name around here again, and you're not going to mention her name anywhere outside of here, either. Understand?"

And as Sean rose to his feet, ignoring his father's hateful sneer and the stale breath above him, swiftly slipping out the front door as fast as he could, he knew he would never mention it; he would do his best to clear it from his mind entirely.

But now, years later in Dr. Cohart's office, Sean had still not managed to clear it away. It drove him crazy to wonder how this memory could just appear out of nowhere, and yet he still felt its truth deep in his soul. Who *was* his real father? There couldn't be two. But at an exponential rate, his memory of the beautiful relationship he had with the father he once knew became increasingly distant, until all he knew was destruction. That was his only reality now.

"Sean, you've—" Cohart paused. He second-guessed his next words.

Sean struggled even harder to conjure a positive memory of his real father as new memories started to creep in. There was a beating after he broke a vase in the kitchen. No—the sound of his mother's car starting up the night she finally left them for good. Then Denise again, with those glistening stab wounds...

Denise's body morphed into Carly's, the lifeless date on the floor of his Brooklyn apartment. And now Sean was remembering the woman he chopped to bits underneath the train tracks behind his condo in—where was that again? Buena Park? Yeah, when he lived further west—and there were so many others, Sean knew. He knew there were. And he knew that by thirty-eight years old, more than twenty of those victims had conglomerated into his life's work.

"You've shared two memories now, neither of which I can wrap my head around," Dr. Cohart continued, "Sean, I know your father; we grew up together. He and your mother have been happily married for nineteen years. And you've barely started your senior year of high school here in Burlington; you've never lived on your own in New York City..."

Cohart paused, but continued, "...have you ever even had a girlfriend? Could a bad experience be triggering some of these—"

Fucking bitch must pay...

The metallic shine appeared on everything again; everywhere Sean looked, it clouded his vision. It was all shining and glistening, like a pale gray finish he couldn't escape.

Dr. Cohart didn't get it. He didn't understand, and he didn't care. He needed to pay, too.

Sean reached into his backpack, feeling around for anything that might be there: a knife, a hammer, a gun, anything? Did he have anything? Was that even something he would ever carry with him?

Yes, a handgun. It was in there. A 9mm, a Glock 19. Where did he get it?

He looked at Cohart, eyeing his prey as he fastened a tight grip around the handle of the gun in his bag. The liquid metal effect had engulfed more than half of Cohart's face like a blanket of ooze. Now there was more of it covering his dark brown cardigan sweater and the thighs of his gray slacks.

Unable to view the actual expression on Cohart's face as he pulled the gun out, Sean pointed it directly at his head and fired. The haze of violent memories, paranoia, hate, and fear seemed to provide a muting effect over the noise of the gunshot, barely startling Sean as he watched the bullet rip through his doctor's skull.

A crimson explosion painted the bookshelf behind Sean's victim, quickly blanketed by the metallic silver that engulfed the room. Blood, chunks of brain, and skull fragments hurled through the air in a line drive at the wall. Like a shining statue with nearly half a head, Cohart's lifeless body flung backward, tipping over his armchair as he crashed to the floor.

Sean dropped the gun back into his backpack and quickly exited. He knew exactly where he needed to go.

Back to the source. The source of all this pain.

***

Not even two decades earlier, his parents had both met there, working lame but eventually sentimental high school summer jobs: The optimism and joy that centered The Pound was a staple of Sean's childhood. It was not just a still-going-strong local landmark to grab one of the cheapest and best burgers in town, it was a magical place in his family history.

It was.

As Sean paced rapidly across concrete squares covered in that multiplying silver ooze, he had the same destination as one that he had after school with friends on many occasions. Now he faced the destination alone, and there were no aspirations of good times ahead. Instead, the feeling was desperation, a necessity to confront the potential cause of this crumbling world around him. Fear and hopelessness were the emotions that now circled above The Pound's parking lot.

And this substance lay in the middle of a town now painted with that glistening shine. Sean still had no idea what the hell it was. Was it even in physical form? Was this substance based in reality?

No, this was an illusion. The image came back again as Sean tried to avoid stepping in the puddles of liquid metal that he knew were, quite possibly, not actually there.

The image of the puddle in the middle of the parking lot flashed back again. It had glistened in a way that seemed to speak to him.

Where do you think you're going, Sean...

You best come look at this. Your whole life depends on it...

But Sean's life was rotting because of this...thing, this substance—this puddle that looked like a shiny oil spill. When he had first looked down at it, he saw a reflection of someone he knew was himself. But for a brief moment, not even half a second, he received a painful and shocking feeling of utter unfamiliarity, an uncomfortable split millisecond of a void. He didn't recognize who he was.

Then it ended. He shook it off. He didn't even have a chance to think to himself, *"Why the fuck am I staring at this puddle of glistening oil on the ground?"* before he was off on his way again. It was like it hadn't happened.

And Sean now had blood on his hands. Forget the random memories that he couldn't recognize despite how despicably real they seemed. Forget the trauma he all of a sudden recalled that couldn't be confirmed by the known timeline of his life. Forget Carly—poor Carly...

35

Forget those memories, regardless of how or why they kept creeping up. He had fresh blood on his hands from an incident that had just happened. This wasn't an unknown memory. He knew he had blown Cohart's brains out all over the place. There was no need to be confused by a memory of it. It was real. Murder was real.

What threat had Cohart posed? Why was there a need to take that Glock out of his backpack and pull the trigger?

Glock? I don't know the first thing about guns...I'm not even old enough to buy one...

Nothing made sense. Not his recent actions, not his past actions, not his present. Only one thing made sense—the near future.

Sean would go back to where he saw that substance on the ground, the same substance that was engulfing more and more of his entire field of vision by the second. At this point, it was harder to find a person, place, or object that wasn't covered in it—but maybe there were answers back at the source.

As he approached an intersection he could barely recognize enough to know its cross streets, Sean made a sharp right and darted in the direction of the historic hot dog stand—about a hundred feet away. A chilling thought appeared, one that could have come to him a lot sooner had he been thinking logically and not in a state of sheer insanity.

How am I going to recognize a small puddle on the ground when this stuff is everywhere now...

Fuck. Fuck. Fuck.

Fucking bitch must pay...

No, not now. Stop. I didn't do anything. I didn't kill her. I didn't kill the others. I never became this. I didn't experience a violent childhood. My father didn't kill Denise. My father is a nice man. My mother never left us...

By sheer willpower alone, Sean shook away the storm of trauma blazing around in his head and maintained his focus. He flattened his feet to a halt at the foot of the curb. He was standing in the parking lot of The Pound.

It was exactly as he had just considered it would be. Still, there was no way to tell if the oil spill was really there or not. The entire parking lot was now covered in it; it all looked the same. But he had to see this through as much as he could. Sean approached the specific section of the lot where he had initially spotted the puddle a week earlier.

As he drew nearer, another boy was walking out of the restaurant, headed towards the same spot. He was closer to it. He was a few paces closer to the puddle.

Miraculously, Sean could see that the puddle was there now. It was barely distinguishable as it resembled every other ounce of that terrifying substance, but it was just isolated enough to where it could be recognized. It beckoned him but seemed to also call out to the other young man approaching it on the opposite side of the parking lot.

No, dude... Don't look at it...

Sean wondered if the boy could see the rest of the liquid around him, making it confusing for him, too, to spot the lone puddle.

No, of course, he can't see it. That's my reality, not his. And only mine. Right?

The boy was within mere feet of the puddle now, glaring his eyes toward it with innocent fascination. But he seemed exempt from any type of metallic shine, which had now covered virtually everything Sean could see at this point. It was like the boy was impervious to a virus consuming everything else in its path. At that moment, Sean realized who was in front of him and drew the gun from his backpack.

You represent the version of me that no longer exists, the fantasy pulled over my eyes. You have confused me and wasted my time this entire week...

These dark, conflicting thoughts invaded Sean's head and caused him to feel an intense rage that reminded him of what he felt in the hallway with Carly. He observed the vision of himself staring down at the puddle from a few feet away and stopped advancing to meet him there. Instead, he tightened his stance and brought the gun out, pointing it straight ahead.

No. Stop it. You don't want to kill him. That's the real you. Don't do this...

Sean loosened his grip on the handle. Was he really going to shoot this boy? Something didn't seem right.

Do it. Then you can live your life as you know it to be. No more confusion. No more questions. No more lies...

The force of hatred, anger, and confusion pulled the trigger. A bullet went soaring through the mid-afternoon air and tore through the boy's skull—a perfect shot. Sean knew it was over as he watched him fling backward with a sickening speed and smack down onto the pavement. Sean was real now, as a splash of the boy's dark red blood painted the concrete. Sean had returned.

And the metallic shine disappeared in an instant. The moment that bullet had blasted from his gun, Sean could see the world fresh again.

"What are you doing?!" a woman screamed at him. He turned towards her and shot another round that hit her in the shoulder and sent her soaring. He walked a little closer and fired again at her trembling body on the ground in front of him; the force of the bullet impacting her skull caused her brain to splatter across the parking space. No witnesses now, at least not any that were close enough to see him clearly.

Sean turned and ran back towards the direction he came from, just to get away from the scene. But his panic had ended. He was running to escape punishment, and with each stride, he felt zero remorse. He felt nothing but relief.

He took off his hoodie, rolled up his jeans, and used the sweat that had accumulated on his forehead and on the top of his head to mess up his hair. He took off the backpack around his shoulder and dumped it into a trashcan. Sean cut through a nearby yard and began walking through a neighborhood he no longer recognized as a part of his hometown. He enjoyed a moment of peace and quiet.

As he exited the neighborhood a few minutes later, he saw an office that sparked a split second of a memory. Not even a memory. An ever-so-brief familiarity...

"DAVID H. COHART, CLINICAL SOCIAL WORK," the sign in front said.

Weird. Where do I recognize that from?

Brushing off a meaningless instance of déjà vu, Sean passed the office and walked toward a nearby bus station. He wasn't sure where he was, exactly, but he knew one thing for sure—later that night, he had plans with a girl he'd met in front of the library, and he had to get back to New York.

Almost every other day, I drive by a run-down dive bar isolated on Route 31 that looks like a place where people go to die. Without any judgment, I can assume that's not far off. It is a privilege to pass a prison and merely wonder what it's like inside before moving on to another thought.

"The Sacrifice" is a miserable world that I would never willingly subject myself to. I do not need authenticity to know that the pain inside four walls is real. Still, I wanted to take it a step further and write about a man who discovered a chance to do something beautiful within his abhorrent life.

THE SACRIFICE

I stumbled, as I so often did, out the front door and right over to my car, a beat-up '98 Oldsmobile Cutlass that had gotten me to and from my most common destination every night of every week. It was the place I was headed to now, the only place that felt like home after 8:00 PM.

She was still screaming. I could hear it up until I shut the door of the old piece of junk and started the ignition, *"LEAVE...LEAVE LIKE YOU ALWAYS DO, YOU FUCKING PIECE OF—"*

Whatever—this was nothing new. I felt calloused as I wondered which one of us was growing more sick of this routine—her, without any doubt—I know every one of these nights, this ongoing spectacle is all because of me. I am the one who is wrong in these back and forths. But that doesn't change anything at this moment; I'm pissed off, I'm tired, I'm drunk, and I need to go somewhere better.

"Better" is not Stormy's, but you couldn't convince me of that. No, not on any day of the week. I was always going to find "better" at Stormy's, the only place that felt like home after 8:00 PM.

***

Down Route 26, past the Walmart, and then past the old Biggins Pancake House—way past—you'll find that the highway thins down to a two-lane road with nothing but dust and dirt on either side. The grass fades away, the stores disappear, and civilization seems to look at you and wave good-bye...not the other way around. There should be a "Now Leaving Oberton"

41

sign at some point, but you surely won't find one. Make no mistake about it, you're still in town; you're just no longer really a part of it.

On the right, just before the entrance ramp to Interstate 4, lies Stormy's Tavern. I really can't begin to explain the appeal of it, you just sort of have to be a person like me; few are. But the few that I would consider pathetic enough to say so, join me a few nights a week, sometimes more, to drown our sorrows and revel in past, present, and future mistakes. Each night: a reminder; and Stormy's makes sure we never forget our place in this world.

It stands crooked and decrepit, much like the patrons inside—with warped and splintered boards forming its frail skeleton. There's a neon light hanging above the entrance that is so dim and flickery it nearly forfeits its purpose; I wish they'd just turn the damn thing off already, or simply fix it at some point. That ghastly, expiring glow is not without its charm, though—if you want to call it that. It so closely mirrors the life that is left of Stormy's customers behind the doors, almost serving to forewarn you of what you might find inside.

The place smells as stale dive bars tend to: a scathing, yet comforting, cocktail of cigarettes, rotting wood, and the breath of every alcoholic you've ever found yourself sitting next to on the bus. When I said it was the only place that felt like home to me after a certain point in the evening, I meant it.

"Start with two, Marty."

I slumped in my stool as my old pal got my drinks ready without asking. You know you're a lost cause when, one: you know the bartender's name and consider them a friend; two: you don't need to tell them what you're having. But I was in no denial of who I was. Every time I opened my mouth, or experienced one second without distraction, all the reminders of this trainwreck inside me became my neverending plague.

We usually call Martin Abramowicz "Marty," but occasionally an older friend will spill into the bar and address him as "Abey," which we always share a cough-laden chuckle over. As you might guess after observing Marty's consistently frazzled demeanor behind the bar, he has been at this a long fucking time. I once asked him if he owned Stormy's, to which he began to ramble on about a "son of a bitch" who "fucked him six ways to Sunday," "back in '68 before any of youse were even in grade school." Somehow I always got the feeling he might still be bitter about whatever went down... but yeah, he had been there forever, it seemed. He was a true veteran.

As bitter old Marty poured my gin and tonics behind the bar, I rested my forearms on the pale, honey-finished oak surface in front of me and thought about Shelley. No doubt, she was furious and I wasn't sure if she'd be there when I got back this time. I hadn't been sure of that in a long, long time. I doubted if I even had a reason for returning home each time I left for the evening. But of course, I had one—the only reason.

I pictured her in her toddler-sized bed, snuggling her pink cotton blanket. Only seconds earlier muttering "Lights out, Dada," which is our thing we say before I shut the door, in her little, quiet, half-asleep voice. And as I imagined her turning on her other side, her head hanging slightly off the edge of the pillow, I felt like an even bigger piece of shit than I thought possible.

With that, I took my first sip of the evening.

***

The night reached 10:30 PM in what seemed like not even a passing moment. I don't lose my composure anymore when I do this to myself—not even gradually. I think at this point, I just continue to survive. You survive until you die, both at the same time. It ain't living, but it was the only way I knew how to at least tolerate my existence. Each hour of each night dissolved like sugar in water.

I had seen a lot of bullshit go down at that bar over the years. Drama. Plenty of fights. A couple of overdoses, even. More ambulances left Stormy's than I could count on two hands; maybe even my toes. But hell, there were even some good times: partying; women; celebrations, in that ludicrous sort of way that young up-and-coming alcoholics delude themselves to participate in as they force smiles and dredge through a caricature of an energy that eventually becomes second nature.

That was twenty-something years ago, however. My generation has faded into the same lazy and tiresome kind of misery that resonated here before us; we were approaching the end. And when the regulars at a shady rotting tavern on the very edge of town start to become old, no one willingly follows in their footsteps.

The next generation always gets sucked in—we *end up* here, brutally unconscious of our injurious journey. This little haven of failure, however, might as well be the land that time forgot. At that point, myself and the old-timers were the only people keeping it there; it was looking like I might be one of the last of that "next generation" before every one of us was buried in the past.

So tonight was like any other: quiet. Rock groups like Styx and The J. Geils Band played faintly on the speakers, just loud enough for Marty to make the occasional bitter comment about the songs from behind the bar. That was, until the door creaked open, and a man I hadn't seen in months flooded through the entrance.

A condescending sigh from Marty pierced the dead silence: "Ah, shit."

I looked up from my stagnant gaze at the cocktail in front of me and turned my head towards the door. Leland's presence was hardly welcome, yet his painfully fitting demeanor to Stormys' culture was undeniable. We couldn't turn him away. To grace these parts was to accept an unfavorable clientele. At the end of the day, we were no better.

"Abes! Get me a Coors on the house!"

Even Marty knew this man was a crazy old kook. And those you might call "normal" would consider Marty to be just the same. But Marty's bitterness, neuroticism, and sheer distaste for humanity still could never amount to anything that sunk as low as the redneck lowlife scumbaggery that was Leland King. We knew it, too. Compared to this stain on society, Marty was a dear old grandfather. And we loved him, anyway.

"First two are free if you shut your damn mouth, King," Marty bellowed. "We got a deal?"

We never could tell if Leland even needed the drinks. Any normal person wouldn't set foot in a bar at close to 11:00 PM without a thirst. But this man, this...cretin, very well could have just been bored as shit, looking for anyone he might be able to terrorize for a few hours. Needless to say, I always suspected the latter from him any time he walked through the doors.

I must specify—I never knew Leland, really. And looking at him now, I didn't have the history that Marty, or the others in here, had with him. I spoke earlier of my generation. Well, keep in mind, there was that generation before mine who were truly rotting their final teeth away in this dump. They made me feel young. At least, they should have. Their example should have led me towards a moment of clarity more than a decade earlier. Instead, I accepted an identical fate and continued to rest comfortably on their sinking ship.

Leland kept to himself and, as the others would tell me, spent most of his day in his run-down shack deep in the outskirts of Oberton. He no doubt suffered from mental illness, or perhaps it was just a reflection of mounting decades within toxic surroundings. Rarely did he visit Stormy's, or anywhere else in town. Even when considering the local lore, most folks seemed to know very little about Leland, other than Marty, of course. As I always assumed of most of these old townies, Marty seemed to have some sort of bent history with Leland. It was only from the times he decided to invade the bar and ruin our already hopeless evenings, the ignorant nuisance he was, that I got even a glimpse into what this man was about. And as stated, it was rare.

There was silence as Leland cracked open his can of Coors after parking himself at the counter. He was seemingly willing to comply with Marty's request to take his free beer and settle down, something we all knew wouldn't last long. And after not even two minutes, he spoke.

"Never'll guess what I found..."

His delivery was so quiet that it posed no challenge to drown out and ignore. But as he repeated the statement a second time, not louder but slower and with syllables more clearly emphasized, I realized Leland was talking right to me. After excruciating hesitation, I replied. "What, King?"

I had reached the point in the evening where I was just beginning to feel numb, it was like nothing mattered, and I was where I needed to be. Whatever was waiting for me at home was on pause; as long as I stayed away, I wouldn't have to face it.

"Never'll guess what I found...come with me, and I'll *show* ya."

I turned my stare back to my glass, concentrating on the stale mixture of toxins left inside. I ignored Leland again and took another sip.

"You think you're better 'an me, you son of a bitch...you think..."

I continued to let Leland's rambling gurgle of a voice trail off, blocking him out entirely. I was in no mood for this. No mood at all.

***

Come with me and I'll show ya.

It was nearing 11:30 PM and I felt an annoyance building with each damp, molting leaf squishing underneath my work boots. With every step I took further away from the bar, I felt more and more disappointed with myself. And, as I stared straight ahead at the dirt-covered, sweat-drenched backside of my deplorable colleague, I could feel my evening fully lowering to the standards of a miscreant.

By the time I decided to entertain, and in some ways patronize, Leland King's ambitions of impressing an insignificant local, I had already found myself feeling apathetic and willing enough to go along with whatever opportunity might've presented itself to me, no matter how absurd or pointless. I knew all along that I wanted nothing more than to be left alone, so I could finish my night and stumble my way back out to my Cutlass and risk the dangers of darting down Route 26 inebriated. Still, I tend to lack conviction at this point in the evening, so I can no longer rely on myself. Not until the next morning, at least. And then it's back to life.

Instead, I'd now face whatever Leland had in store for me. But try to imagine my level of disassociation at this time—a lack of excitement, zero focus, a slight bit of anticipation if you could call it that—and you could maybe then accurately describe where my energy was on this potentially cursed mini-journey.

Christ, am I really fucking following Leland King across the muddy outskirts of Oberton right now?

"You still behind me, Jimmy?"

My name's not even fucking Jimmy...

"Yeah, King, I'm still here. How much longer?"

"Just around the bend, Jimmy Boy. Wait 'til you see this shit."

In the Midwest, temperatures this time of night in September aren't exactly what I'd consider comfortable. The summer is just beginning to cool itself into Fall, yet there is not a hint of crispness in the humid air. Such

46

is a metaphor for life's miserable aura: just because the sun isn't directly blistering your skin doesn't mean you aren't aware of its heat.

I trotted behind Leland, breathing in that stale air as my exhausted lungs began to fail me. It couldn't have been much longer now, because Oberton wasn't that big of a town, even considering the time it took to get to Stormy's from where most considered to be civilization. This old man was pushing eighty. If he could handle this trek, so could I.

Without another word of confirmation, I knew we were approaching our destination. I could make out the only residence within miles; it was in the form of a run-down, white-wooded shack just past a line of pine trees leading our path. No doubt this was once a farmhouse, just as isolated as rural farmhouses always are. A younger Leland could have suffered a lot here, and no one would have ever known—or cared to know.

Moments like these, drunk or not, made you sift through all of your bullshit, your selfish, narcissistic world of constant dismay, and inch towards further appreciation of what you had. Was it all so bleak by comparison? Images of my single-family home flashed before me: Shelley and I, during happier times—and my beautiful angel, resting safely in her toddler bed.

Lights out, Dada...

All of that good stuff, there. Here, I stared forward at a living hell thirty feet ahead. A worthless excuse for home. Trapped inside, among desolate memories from a life of true pain. I had things just fine; I just chose to fuck it all up.

What, in God's name, are you fucking doing out here, Jimmy?

I interrupted my depressive, drunken epiphany to chuckle to myself, reflecting on my current impairment and, therefore, my ability to accidentally address myself as my Leland-appointed alter-ego.

I guess we're in it for the long haul tonight, Jimmy Boy. Stop obsessing over yourself and go see what Leland's got back here.

"This way," Leland demanded, "around back."

I followed him over to a pair of battered wooden basement doors that barely served their purpose as they had rotted clear away to expose most of a dark concrete stairwell that led underground. Leland proceeded to aggressively pull open the right side with every ounce of his frail might. I helped him with the other side.

Though pitch black in my view, the unmistakable sound of scampering footsteps, along with something else I wasn't completely sure of, managed to chill me to my very bones. It was then that I noticed the booze starting to wear off; in fact, it might have fully worn off. Regardless, I don't think intoxication could dissolve the sheer terror of what I had just seen.

"What the fuck was that, King?!"

"Ahhh, see? See? I told ya. I told ya!"

"Who was that? You don't have any family here—"

"Follow her on down there, Jimmy!"

This man is absolutely crazy, I thought. And more so, what had I really expected anyway? Did I not expect to see the shadow of something human scurry away into the depths of Leland's horrifying, ancient cellar the second we peered open those doors? Was it so hard to believe?

"I'm heading back, King. Fuck you—this is nuts..."

With a rapid motion, he aggressively clutched my arm; his elderly lack of strength proved irrelevant. It was the long and jagged, unkempt fingernails digging into my flesh that sent painful shockwaves up through my arm and down my spine.

"No no, see, I wanna show ya!" he pleaded insistently. "I wanna show ya what I got down there!"

With unimaginable, determined force, he lugged me down the stairs, nearly toppling me to the ground as we reached the bottom of the cellar. A faint light from underneath the upstairs kitchen doorway shone just enough of a glow on the prisoner who was shivering in the corner of the basement.

"What...what the fuck, Leland..." I said, trembling and sober. I could barely see who was standing a few feet before me, as they were merely a silhouette blended into an already dingy background.

"I caught me a spider, Jimmy Boy."

I looked at Leland in disbelief, still struggling to process what I had gotten myself into. "Who is it, Leland? What the fuck did you do?"

"You ain' never believe it neither, son. I'm sittin' on my porch, not more 'an three hours ago, and I hear a rustlin', right behind that big ole pine tree by the mailbox."

He paused, and I said nothing.

"And the bitch was just sittin' there! Knelt down by the tree trunk, mumblin' at the dirt!" He let out a cackle that sounded like nails on a chalkboard. I couldn't speak.

"So you see, she was just sittin' there. No idea where she came from—looked like she just appeared outta nothin'. But she's mine now!" His cackling intensified, and I began to realize that I was not only dealing with the mentally insane; Leland King was worse than that.

I had to turn away from his disgusting, toothless grin. I gathered the willpower to peer back over to the corner and then took a few steps forward. As I got closer, I could see her huddled down, her hands covering her face. As if Leland could read my mind, a flashlight clicked on and I could then see her much better. Still freshly traumatized, the first thing I noticed was a dried stream of blood trickling down from the old woman's ear to her arm, then her bony wrist, and finally to her fingertips.

"Did you...hit her?" I asked, sneering back toward Leland's looming outline in the darkness.

"'Course, son. She might've escaped hadn't I, right?"

My shock turned into anger and quickly grew; I felt urges familiar to me from so many past brawls. Those booze-fueled rages directed at all of the wrong people in my life, and those emotions that led to mistakes that led to victims. But, at this moment, I knew for the first time that I was on the right side of the hatred.

"Now," he continued, taking a step toward me, "She looks to me like one of them old Jews, uglier than anyone you or I seen, that's for sure. I dunno where she came from, but I ain't never gotten this kinda chance before."

His opportunities to smooth this over were long gone, and he was either too insane or stupid to know any better. Or, there was the chance he was deliberately trying to make this worse. My money was on the former.

"My daddy got to take out plenty of 'em when I was just a young'n that ain't know any better; and now you're gonna help me finish the job. You're the lucky one tonight, Jimmy. I'm gonna share the fun with ya. She's ours now."

As if our senses were aligned, both of us looked at the plywood-topped work table to our right. Leland's skeleton-like hand reached over towards a Colt .38 pistol lying right on the edge. My brain froze in panic, but my body reacted; I was alarmed to see his hand clamp down on the weapon's handle. Despite my shock, I somehow performed a precise and swift lunge where my foot knocked his elbow into the side of the plywood—a kick that was miraculously timed and perhaps saved the old woman's life. Leland let out a painful shriek; it was a sound that was somehow more unsettling than his callous laughter from a moment prior.

Before I knew anything more, Leland's back was to the floor with a mushroom cloud of dust kicked up into the air. I'd punted his chest with sheer ferocity, more than likely shattering the deteriorating ribcage of a man whose time had truly ended decades ago.

"You...son of a...bitch...Jimmy...what the..." he belted out through gasps of agony.

"My name's not fucking Jimmy, you piece of shit."

"We were gonna...you and I were gonna..."

I wasn't willing to hear another delusional word from the parasite beneath me. "I'm glad I get to put you out of your misery, Leland."

And without another thought, my right workboot rose several feet up into the air and stomped down onto Leland's neck with the force of a triggered mousetrap. With zero remorse, entirely encompassed by my own maddened fury, I pushed downwards with everything I had as I felt every bone in his spinal cord crackle and crunch into the pavement. The image of blood, darker than the darkest crimson in the scarcely lit basement, spurting from his throat and out through his lifeless mouth, was in and out of my head in milliseconds. During that moment, when Leland King's saga of failure and misfortune ended, all I could focus on was the excruciating headache that was suddenly apparent to me.

***

She clearly couldn't understand a word I tried to say. Through quiet and timid sobs of distress, the old woman just looked at me—helpless, like an orphaned child.

"Let's see, he's gotta have something in here, uh..." I mumbled to myself as I rummaged through empty mason jars and chipped ceramic plates in Leland's cupboard.

Enough cockroaches were scurrying across the filthy linoleum of the kitchen floor to infest ten more households. And, somehow, the first floor of that dilapidated old farmhouse was even colder than the murky basement below. The stove top ignited just fine, so the heat definitely wasn't turned off. A broken furnace could've easily been the problem. Needless to say, Leland King had lived in squalor, possibly for decades.

After moments of rummaging through junk, I was able to scavenge a dirty mug, a rusted saucepan, and a crumpled box of expired Lipton lemon tea pouches; it would have to do.

"Okay, uh, I'm making you some tea—" I said, pointing to the water I had started to boil and making a drinking hand motion, "warm...it will warm you right up."

She was already wearing multiple dusty layers of coats and sweaters, like a walking burlap sack. As I watched her hunch over the round table in the corner of the room, shivering and whimpering, I recalled her ancient smell when I helped her up the cellar steps. The only way I could describe such a smell was that she reeked of a different time period.

"Mój wnuk," she said, all of a sudden. "Mój wnuk. Filip. *Filip*."

The pain in her voice was dreadful to hear; I didn't have a clue how to respond. And the second the water came to a boil and bubbles started to rise to its surface, I quickly poured a cup and served it to her.

"Filip," she repeated. "Mój wnuk. Mój wnuk. Wrócić...wrócić."

Filip? A name? I wasn't good with languages, but this sounded Eastern European to me. She looked European. Leland had said she was likely Jewish. I did the only thing I knew I could do. The fact that I had such a resource to consider was a miracle.

***

As I waited in the next room, sober as a judge, I felt like I was long past the point of losing my goddamned mind. *What in the fuck was going on here?*

The old woman's whimpering had tamed, and I occasionally peered through the entryway to the kitchen to see her gently sipping on her tea. She still shivered, however, and I could tell that it wasn't because of the temperature.

It had been about an hour and a half, according to the clock on the oven—an hour and a half since I had left Stormy's to throw myself into this mess. The bar wouldn't close for another few hours still, and the fate of this evening now rested in the hands of this grumpy old misanthrope.

As fate would have it so far, I was turning out to be somewhat of a hero. I didn't know who I was saving, or why, but Leland had intended to cause serious harm to an innocent human being. Now he no longer could.

Christ, there is a body downstairs.

Then I reminded myself that this was the rural Midwest; this was Oberton, Michigan. Sure, the police would come. Leland would be carried away in a body bag like any other lifeless clump of flesh would be. But no one would care; and when no one cares, no one investigates. At least, not around here they don't.

Me...a *hero*. I don't know if the forced sobriety had truly discombobulated my brain, or if I just couldn't help but see the irony. I laughed out loud at the thought of it.

Shelley doesn't have a hero in her life. She has me.

Waiting and waiting, with only more time to wait, I began to torture myself in reflection. Make no mistake about it, I was no hero. I was an abusive drunk with what was now appearing to be a shred of a conscience.

Does a decent life-saving act preceded by countless neglected familial responsibilities really deserve praise? Which side of the balance do you weigh...

I hated Shelley often. There had been times I felt no remorse listening to her cries, pacing back and forth with beer in hand, yelling insults at her from the other room. Viewing her as a thorn in my side, a relentless source of inconvenience and judgment. The wife I never wanted, the mother to my—

No. I was the monster. It always led back to the same epiphany, whether filtered through drunken self-pity or stone-cold sobriety...

It was me I hated. Time and time again. Me.

And villainizing Shelley wasn't the only lie I continuously told myself. There was another.

My little angel in her bed. I thought of her again, and my attempts to shield her from my nightmare of tyranny. It was not her problem. It was Shelley and I's problem, and it was our secret. Our conflict. Our growing mess in our lives. What our little one couldn't hear or see...couldn't hurt her. And therefore, she would turn out fine. I made sure of it...

The sudden knocking on Leland King's front door pounded through my ears and into my mind like a battering ram. No more time to reflect. He's here.

"What in the fuck is going on?"

"I'm hoping you can tell me," I said, holding the flimsy screen door open for Marty as he barged his way past me. "That's why I called the bar."

"It's been a shitty fucking night," Marty grumbled. "I'm surprised Leland's even got a working phone. Where is he?"

"Marty, he's dead," I said. "He's dead in the cellar. I had to kill him."

With the slightest pause, Marty shrugged and said, "About time."

Endearing qualities don't come in the same form when you're a Stormy's patron. When it came to someone like Marty, I needed his hard-headed and heartless apathy at that moment. Fewer things could have offered a measurable sense of calm.

I led Marty into the kitchen, where the old woman still sat. Lowering my voice, I put a hand gently on my old friend's right shoulder and huddled closer to him.

"King said this woman just appeared behind the bushes near his mailbox. He thought she was a Jew...he was going to kill her, Marty. You grew up in Eastern Europe, didn't you? Is there any chance you could understand her?"

"East Germany, near Poland. I'd have to hear what she's saying first, wouldn't I?" he haughtily whispered back.

"Talk to her, please."

With a dirty look that could make a sociopath cower in shame, Marty turned to face the old woman.

"Talk to me."

Her wrinkled face kept her beady eyes half-shut in a permanent squint, but she opened them further and began to repeat herself, "Mój wnuk. Mój wnuk. Wrócić...wrócić."

Marty's reaction shocked me in a way I wouldn't expect from him—his eyes saddened, and perhaps for the first time, I noticed compassion emanating from his gaze. His tone shifted from disdain to tender consideration as he spoke back to her. She opened her eyes with mild eagerness and began to recite what appeared to be a thorough explanation.

When she stopped again, Marty turned back to me with a benign expression that convinced me he had transformed into a different person.

"She's a Polish Jew alright. I haven't spoken Yiddish since I was a kid, but I understand what she's saying—you aren't going to believe this."

I looked at him in amazement.

"Her name is Dorotka. She doesn't know how she got here," he continued, "she was trapped, underneath a safe house, with her grandson. Her grandson didn't arrive here with her; he must still be there."

"Safe house? What...still be where...?"

"I think she's—" he paused, perhaps in disbelief himself, "I think she's from the past."

***

As Dorotka sipped on her tea, she continued shivering while softly murmuring to herself here and there. I looked at Marty, waiting for him to respond to me; there had been a solid minute of silence.

The empathetic twinkle in his eyes remained and my initial shock had waned. The feeling of acceptance I needed to normalize this notion that

Martin Abramowicz could harbor anything but distaste for another human being—it finally made sense. Despite the miserable life I chose for myself, and the pain I irresponsibly shared with so many over the years, I still believed in people; I still had faith in their hearts and Marty was a person like any other. Seemingly, the heartfelt, imploring tale of an old Polish woman, who was apparently a time traveler, was enough to crack open his bitter exterior and expose that side of himself he almost always refused to embrace.

"I think you're fucking nuts," he said to my immediate surprise, "what are you gonna do? Save the world? Play God? It's been a long night, son. I don't have any more time for this." Sighing in shame, as if he wished he could trust in the practicality of my plan, he crept up from his crouching position and started to head for the door.

"Wait, Marty. Wait," I pleaded. "What else is she going to do? Who else is going to help her?"

"No one is, son. I have to tell you, if what she says is true, it's strange and unfortunate."

"That's an understatement, Marty. Come on, now. We're all she has."

"*You're* all she has. I'm heading home. You got your translation services for the night. You don't need me anymore."

Apparently, the concept of moral support had become lost on my old friend, despite whatever inkling of kindness he had begun to show. But he was right. I didn't need anybody else at this point.

Without so much as a "*good luck*" or even an ill-fated attempt at "*don't do it, son*", he was out of sight. I shouldn't have been surprised.

And once again, I had no way to communicate with Dorotka.

***

That smell of a different time period was back, and it chilled my bones most uncomfortably. To say I had never traveled fifty years back in time before wouldn't have been enough of an explanation for the unsettling confusion I was experiencing. This was utterly horrifying.

With a cat burglar's prudence, I tip-toed across the dark crawlspace. The slabs of wood lying across the dirt floor rattled with each baby step I took. Determined as I was, I could feel my confidence crumbling. I had never really succeeded at anything—how was I going to succeed at this?

Burglar...

I am a burglar—I have stolen much in my lifetime. Bouts of addiction had taken me to shameful levels of betrayal towards friends and family, during those moments when one does virtually anything to score. At last, I had a chance to make up for everything I had taken, by giving something back to its rightful owner. Something undeniably more important than anything material.

The time portal required no finesse at all. I had brushed around the area Leland had described, where he apparently had found Dorotka, and frantically looked for something that wasn't visibly there. Then, all of a sudden, I was somewhere else. There were no flashing lights—no "whooshing" sounds, or any feeling akin to slipping through a wormhole. It was unlike anything I had ever experienced and, yet, there was almost nothing to it.

Startled by the confusion of a new, foreign environment, however, I had lost my balance and stumbled right onto a stack of old paintings that were conveniently encased in jagged metal frames. Immediately upon cutting my arm:

So this is what sobriety feels like.

I desperately needed a drink and, at the same time, I wasn't convinced I'd ever have another. There was no time for that now, anyway, I came here for one reason.

The fear electrifying my veins was absolutely unrelenting. The beads of sweat forming all over my body were impossible to ignore as I looked around.

The only light I had was seeping deliberately through a single crack in the floor above as if it lacked permission to assist me. I squinted and peered around the room.

There was only a stack of boxes staring at me, overflowing with what looked like clothing from the 1940s. They urged me to go back, warning me of whatever danger was afoot. Helpless and desperate, I struggled to locate the young child.

Suddenly, loud and harsh footsteps pounded the floor upstairs, and I began hearing voices that were faint at first but growing louder; they were shouting in German. The chilling accuracy of every film portraying Nazis I endured back in the 90s was ringing in my ears, right then and there. Terrified beyond belief, I knew I didn't have much time. Vermin was present.

The atrocities of the world ran through my head. The ignorance of violence and war. The capability of evil. The inevitable downfall of mankind.

And a man who hurts his family...

No. Reflect on your bullshit later. Find her grandson, Jimmy. You're already out of time.

As fate would have it, I may have arrived just in time to rescue this kid from enslavement—but where was he? Was there even anybody here? Was Dorotka crazy?

Still attempting to make as little noise as possible, I hectically crept across the wood slabs and scoped through the darkness in search of anything that might resemble a living being.

A staircase. Directly below the light source from the ceiling. Check behind the stairs, Jimmy...

I roamed around the back of the stairs and, miraculously, tracked him down at last.

Dorotka's grandson was there, behind the stairs, cloaked in the same burlap sack rags that she had been. He was practically buried in cloth, and sitting as still and quiet as a paralyzed mouse. He couldn't have been more than three or four years old, and I could barely even make out a face, let alone eyes. Yet somewhere, somehow, there was an invisible force between us, shrouded in the darkness, that connected me to him as some sort of hero. As we faced each other, I knew he was sure I had arrived for him.

There was no time left for caution. I scampered across the dusty wooden planks, stumbling and determined to remain on my feet. I rushed over to the boy and grabbed him with both arms; I lifted him carelessly and flung us both in the direction of the paintings I had cut my arm on.

In that instant, the door to the cellar flung open and I could hear the officers' boots immediately advancing downwards. It was like the sound of the apocalypse.

I forcefully patted the young boy's quilted lower back as I set him down so his feet were flush with the floor, and then I hurried him toward the spot where I had ended up not more than two minutes earlier. Tripping on my feet directly behind him, we reached our destination and I heard the officers landing at the bottom of the stairs behind me.

I watched Dorotka's grandson disappear into thin air as I hit the concrete wall a millisecond later.

He had made it; I had somehow remained stuck in this nightmarish setting of reality's past.

They say that in the seconds leading up to death, your life flashes before your eyes. All I can confirm is that I was able to have one final stint of reflection and clarity: My little angel tossing around in her bed—fatherless. And yet, another child to be saved from an inevitable life of pain.

As bullets riddled my back, neck, arms, and shoulders, my blood spattered the dirt floor below and I collapsed into a peculiar aura of peace.

Lights out, Jimmy.

When I was a kid, about eight years old, I remember walking back to a classmate's house with him after school one day. There was something really unsettling about his house. I don't remember how I processed things at that age, but I remember feeling like I was in a bad place—like I wanted to go home right away. When his father came into the kitchen a little later that afternoon, I felt that injunction even stronger. Something was very wrong with that family.

Something wasn't safe about that environment. I didn't know what my classmate needed solace from, but I knew he needed it; I saw the fear in his eyes when that man walked in. It's hard to imagine what kinds of things might've happened in that house when I, an uncomfortable guest, wasn't there. A child's intuition is either extremely accurate ... or it means nothing at all.

BEHIND SCOTT'S HOUSE

Behind Scott's house, there was an acre of dead trees and a little stream that led to the river downtown. "It's where I go to escape," he said. I never understood what he meant by that until I stayed the night at his house.

My family and I moved from Buford to Merion Township the summer after second grade. It had felt like the longest summer I had ever experienced for reasons only my subconscious could understand. Deep down, I knew that loneliness lay ahead, and I was hanging on to the very last sliver of my comfort zone. I had a bunch of friends before that summer after second grade ended, and then all of a sudden, I had none. Ironically, the transition barely skipped a beat, and on the first day of third grade, a new friend came along.

Scott wasn't like the other kids I knew before; he was lacking something. I couldn't tell what it was, but I felt it right away. Scott had an emptiness about him, and it made me realize how much I missed my old town. Things were happy in Buford, and Merion Township was like Scott; it was empty and sad.

"I have all of the turtles," he said as he came up beside me, near the area where we hung up our jackets. He pointed to my *Teenage Mutant Ninja Turtles* shirt.

"I only have a few," I said, thinking about the latest of the toys I had acquired.

"I'm Scott," he said, pausing. "Will you come over and play with the turtles today?"

I was lonely and sad in a brand-new town, and my desperation to make friends resulted in immediate acceptance of the request. After school that day, I got off at Scott's bus stop and we walked to his house. As it turned out, he lived only about five minutes away from me.

His house was really small, about half the size of mine. One of the windows out front was broken, and I could see the paint peeling off the wood surrounding it. The grass in the yard was long and looked like the weeds my dad would pull every summer. Walking inside the front entrance to the house, I noticed the screen door was torn, barely holding itself up as it slammed shut behind me with an uncomfortable squeaking sound.

I immediately smelled cigarettes, reminding me of how Scott smelled when I had walked beside him earlier. I coughed after inhaling a cloud of stale smoke that had engulfed the kitchen. A lit cigarette rested in an ashtray on the wooden table in the middle of the room, vertically expelling streams of pale-gray death into the musky air.

"Hi, I'm Derek," I said to the lady standing in front of the sink. She did not answer me, nor did she turn to face me. I sensed either cold apathy or pure obliviousness to my presence, unsure of which instinct to believe. All I could see was the frizzy, light-brown hair on the back of her head and her silky, dark green dress that seemed to melt off of her frail body. Scott had already gone into the next room without speaking to her; I followed him without waiting further for a response.

We entered Scott's room, and I could see it was a mess. Clothes and blankets were strewn about, cookie crumbs and half-eaten sandwiches on plates, and empty cans of RC Cola decorated the bed and floor; some were crushed, and some not. My mom never let me keep my room that way, so I figured Scott must have really cool parents. Still, though, something seemed wrong.

I saw Scott dragging something from under his bed. "This is Sam. That's Bridget," Scott said, pointing to two small turtles crawling around a rectangular metal pan that was filled with shallow water. Scott grabbed a small bottle of turtle food and started sprinkling the flakes onto a puddle in front of Sam. He pointed toward his window, "The rest are by the river."

After a few seconds, "Over by the river," he muttered, "that's where the rest of them are."

***

That night, I couldn't sleep. I was haunted by something I had seen earlier in the afternoon. Or at least what I thought I had seen...

Scott and I had played with his turtles for a bit, and he mentioned the river behind his house, where the rest of his turtles were. I asked why they weren't inside with Sam and Bridget.

"I only play with one or two at a time," Scott said. I didn't quite understand why that was, but I didn't ask.

"The river is where I go to escape," he continued, "so I'll see them later."

At around 4:30 PM, after hanging out in Scott's room for not even an hour, I heard a loud snap followed by the stomping of feet. The sound of the slamming screen door did not alarm me, but the look of fear on Scott's face sent an uncomfortable chill down my spine.

"SCOTTY!! DAMN IT!!" a man's voice bellowed from behind the closed door and into the hallway. "DAMN IT, SCOTTY!! GET OUT HERE."

"Go, Derek," Scott said to me. "Go through the window."

"But Scott—"

"Go home. Now."

He opened his bedroom window, and I climbed out. I didn't understand what was happening, but I was scared, too. I was out of there fast.

As the Fall leaves crunched under my feet while I ran across the front yard and out to the street, I got the urge to go back. What if Scott was in danger? He looked so scared. And I had just left him there.

I had made it about ten feet down the sidewalk when I turned back toward the house. And that's when I saw the woman standing behind the kitchen window, in the same place she was when we first got there after school.

But this time, I was looking at the house from the side. I could see the front of her, and I saw that she did not have a face.

I stopped dead in my tracks, blinking twice to make sure it was real; it was. Even through the hazy view of the screen protecting the open window, I could see she had no eyes, no nose, no mouth. There was only a blank, flat surface of flesh with that same frizzy brown hair sitting atop her head. She wasn't moving.

I turned back the other way and ran down the street toward my new house, my heart failing to recover from the beat it had skipped seconds earlier. I ran fast; faster and faster I ran. At that moment, I was thankful Scott lived only minutes away, but I was also terrified to be so close to what I had just seen.

So late that same night, memories of the afternoon were keeping me awake. Not just the fear in Scott's eyes, or Scott's mother's blank face—well, I thought it was his mother, I don't know who else it could have been—or that horrible stomping sound of Scott's father approaching his room. It was mostly curiosity that prevented me from sleeping. I felt like my afternoon had been cut short. I felt like I was in the middle of unfinished business; it felt like there were answers out there somewhere.

I knew it was wrong to sneak out, but I wasn't going to fall asleep any time soon. I looked at the clock radio beside my bed: 10:08 PM. I should have been asleep hours ago.

My parents will kill me if I go to Scott's house now. It's so late...

But that's exactly what I did, I snuck out of my house and went to Scott's. Part of me was feeding off that curiosity as to what I might find if I went back there. Another part of me wanted to save my new friend from whatever it was that he was so afraid of.

***

I had felt this vibe, this darkness and coldness, the moment I stepped out of my parent's '91 Cruiser when we had first moved into our new house. There was a nurturing I was used to in Buford that was missing from the atmosphere. This was not a home where my neighbors would ever care. They had their own darknesses that consumed them—maybe it was the gray skies towering over our neighborhood, or the lack of a warm, neighborly presence upon our arrival, or simply a childish premonition—I could just sense that I was alone in my dangers, dangers that I had yet to experience but felt would be arriving soon.

As our two-story home stared back at me with welcoming but prejudiced eyes—*who is this nice family moving into such a daunting neighborhood,* those eyes said—I swiftly turned around to face the direction our car had come from. I wanted to turn back time, just a day earlier, to when we were still in Buford. Even as we had slept on the floor of our empty, recently sold house, memories of my community, with its friendship and love, still warmed me like a heavy quilt. Returning the stare at my new home, I simply knew we didn't belong here.

The harshest reality about a dead town is that no one comes looking for you. Merion Township reeked of forced oblivion; I could not rely on a community to watch over me. Some people prefer that. They prefer the forced privacy, the apathy to one's situation. I took it as a ruthless absence of compassion. If Merion Township produced families like Scott's, I was an intruder: an outsider looking in. I was a foreign object, therefore unable to connect with the blood that flowed through the veins of the troubled, the neglected, the abused...

So one week later, on the late evening of my first day of school, here I stood in the neighborhood adjacent to mine. The streets were pitch black for hundreds of feet in front of me. Even the frank unfriendliness of my new neighborhood now seemed closer to beautiful Buford compared to what I endured turning the corner onto Scott's block. Perhaps it was my anxiety, my fear of what I might find over there, that put the idea in my head that Scott's street was even worse than mine.

The faceless mother, the angry father...

From about fifty feet away, I could see there was a light on somewhere after all; it was barely impacting the surrounding blackness. It came from a house I could have sworn was the house I had previously spent my afternoon in. I drew nearer and confirmed it was, in fact, Scott's house. My destination was the sole source of light for the entire block.

The hairs on my arms, neck, and back stood up straight. I felt a chill and shivered. This was such a stupid idea.

My sense of caution told me to slow my pace as I was about to pass by the house just before Scott's. I peered around to the side of his house and located the kitchen window where I had seen the faceless woman earlier that afternoon, beckoning to me like death.

She didn't have a face. Just a blank, flat surface of flesh...

What am I doing here...

A few feet from the kitchen window, toward the back of the house, was a porch step beneath a side door. That's where the source of light was coming from, and there was a woman in front of it—*THE* woman...

Does she have a face...

I swiftly took a step back, using the side of the house next door to hide my view of the porch. Any closer, and she'd be able to see me. I flinched, shivered, and started to panic as I took additional steps backward, prudently distancing myself from the house.

Such a stupid idea. But does she have a face this time...

I swallowed the dry lump in my throat and decided to inch my way toward the house for the second time. Again, peering around to the view of the side porch.

There she was, in the same billowing silk dress, her frizzy hair catching the wind of a near-midnight breeze. She sat this time, both knees pressed up to her chin, clutched tightly by two long, trembling arms.

Does she have a face this time...

That same fleshy blank surface stared straight forward as the woman brought a cigarette up to it, with nothing there to utilize it. The image was so disturbing that I, all of a sudden, convinced myself I was in the middle of a nightmare that I could never hope to wake from.

And at that very second, her face appeared. Instantly, Scott's mother was visible. She was taking a long, shivered drag from her cigarette. The ash end provided some additional lighting to illuminate her face. She looked young, frail, and miserable. She vigorously sucked in the smoke, it simultaneously looked to be her only hope for a life source despite killing her in the most painful, agonizing way. As her wrinkled, palpitating fingers slowly pulled the cigarette from her gray-blue puckered lips, she inhaled a pale gulp of smoke. It rapidly disappeared into her mouth and then into her lungs, like a black hole in space.

Her entire body quivered, and I could tell there was more going on than just her natural reaction to the chill of the night. Scott's mother convulsed as if she was just barely hanging on to some form of self-control—like this was her last shred of hope to keep functioning without collapsing to the ground.

Seconds went by, and I continued to study the image of the woman twenty feet from me. I was able to watch her appear before me for the first time, and I never felt so sorry for another person. I was not able to read her mind; however, I felt like I was entirely inside her head. This was a woman so desperately coping with reality, but so ready to die.

As if the disheartening display of Scott's mother could not get any worse, she began to exhale the smoke from her lungs, dismissing a thick stream of it back into the flow of the wind. Her tired, sad, defeated expression dissolved, and within two seconds, her face was gone again.

She doesn't have a face...

The blank, fleshy surface of nothing continued to stare forward, as I stood twenty feet away, unable to move. I managed to drag my right foot backward, inching toward the sidewalk. The scraping sound that followed as my toe met the concrete was loud enough to stop my heart in panic.

She heard the noise and, in an instant, that face of nothing swiftly jerked forty-five degrees to her right and stared directly at me. The terror I felt in that second caused me to let out the quickest of shrieks as I turned around and began to run. Fast, right out of there; across the street, to the left, down the block...

But my nine-year-old curiosity got the best of me, despite my narrow escape from that freakish scenario I couldn't possibly comprehend. I slowed down, reduced my sprint to a light jog, and, while still moving in the same direction, turned my head to see if Scott's mother was chasing after me.

Oh, how I wish I had not looked...

How I wish I had jolted just another fifty feet further in the direction of my house so I could have reached the next block and turned the corner, away from this place...

Darting toward me was a pale-violet skeletal spirit in the shape of the woman, shifting through the night air and whooshing forward like a train at full speed. The ghastly sillhouette of her silky dress flapped in the breeze, her frizzy hair a stream of lines in the air like the smoke that had risen from her cigarette seconds earlier. Through the transparency of her floating figure, I could see her physical body still sitting on the steps and stuck in place. The face of the spirit was hers, the same face that had appeared when she had inhaled her smoke, and I saw that beautiful young woman with a horrified look of sadness and desperation. She reached out her arm and attempted to grab me with a long, bony hand of purple fingers...

My eyes directly met hers, and I felt an eerie connection as I witnessed the emptiness deep in her soul. As she inched closer toward me and attempted to scream into my face, something held her back. No sound came, and her mouth, the shape of a squiggled oval, began to fade away like the ripples of a puddle. Her face mere inches from mine, her eyes drooped downwards in pathetic defeat, as she sprung backward in a flash. With the same train-like rapidness, the spirit was sucked back into Scott's mother's body that still sat on those steps, blank face and all. Yet she continued staring right at me from that spot.

In my mind, I stayed frozen in that moment forever. But in the physical world, I managed to face forward again, regain my speed, and sprint all the way back to my house.

***

He was sitting by himself, as he always did, just staring down at the blacktop. Children ran past him, kickballs bouncing feet away. A world of excitement and bliss surrounded him like a forcefield, and he was nowhere near it.

I debated whether or not I'd even talk to Scott that day. I wanted to, so desperately. I wanted to ask him what was going on, what he was specifically afraid of, what explanation he might have for everything I had seen.

I was terrified to find out, as I figured whatever was happening at that house was affecting Scott a hundred times as much as it had already affected me. I didn't know if I was prepared to be involved in this any deeper. I thought...maybe I still had a chance to escape.

But I gathered up the courage to go all in and approach Scott with open arms, as my father once taught me a true friend would do.

Even when I was within two feet of him, he didn't look up. I stomped my foot nonchalantly on the ground, attempting to disguise it as just another step. Nothing. Not even the slightest flinch.

"Scott..."

I broke his concentration, ever so slightly. He turned his head none more than a centimeter to the right, stayed in place, and then slowly began to lift his head toward my direction.

"Oh, hey, Derek," he said, softly. "Are you okay?"

I was genuinely surprised to be the one getting asked that. I didn't know how to answer it, because I was about to ask it.

"I'm fine. How are you?"

"Okay. Just thinking about my turtles."

It resonated in me just then. The very few conversations we had had in the last three days, and the turtles. We had only really discussed the turtles. They were all he talked about.

"Scott, I noticed something strange about your mother the other day."

He paused, a combined look of confusion and sadness on his pale gray face. In that moment, he resembled a statue and was just as cold. I needed to turn my head, as it was almost too painful to keep looking at. Instead, I stared and waited.

"What do you mean, my *mother*?"

"She is your mother, isn't she? The woman who was in the kitchen?"

"What?"

By now, he was looking right at me. I couldn't tell if he was confused, sad, or maybe even a little angry now. His eyes were burning, burning with a fire that I felt threatened by. I wanted to step back, away from this confusion.

"Your mother—"

"I live with my dad, Derek."

Scott had not broken his gaze, staring deep into my eyes; it was now intensifying into a death glare. It seemed as if, at any moment, he would stand right up and hit me. Worse—kill me. I was in immediate danger.

"No, Scott, there was a woman—"

"My mom died when I was two. I don't even remember her. It's just me and my dad."

I couldn't tell if he was trying to lie on purpose, or if there was some kind of mistake. I didn't know what to say. But that stare—it continued to burn holes through me. The shy loner who was by himself moments earlier was now amidst a war with his enemy...

Me.

"Get out of here, Derek," he bellowed at me, surely loud enough for other kids to take notice. But none of them were paying attention.

"Scott, I'm sorry, I—"

"Damn it, Derek!" It sounded so familiar. "Damn it, get out of here!"

The rage in his voice, his words, they sounded so eerily familiar.

***

He approached me at the end of the day, right as we were leaving to catch our bus home. I nearly turned in the opposite direction just to avoid another frightening interaction.

"I'm sorry, Derek."

Cautiously, I stayed. There was a calmness about Scott that I hadn't seen earlier. I saw a friend in front of me again.

He continued, "I do have a mother, Derek. That was her in the kitchen that day."

"Then why did you say she died?"

"That's what my dad tells me to say."

Damn it, Scotty...

I truly, truly did not understand. But there was something keeping me from asking why. At least I knew I wasn't going crazy; there was a woman in that kitchen. She was also sitting on that porch, and I knew what happened after that...

"Alright, Scott. Well..."

I was about to bring it up, but I couldn't.

"Do you want to have a sleepover on Friday?" he asked, abruptly. "I think I saw that *The Terminator* is playing on HBO."

The thought of a full night at Scott's sent a chill through my body, and I relived that moment on his street all over again: the spirit of Scott's mother attempting to leave her body and scream at me as I stood frozen in terror. I imagined myself there again, that following weekend, and it made me sick to my stomach.

Yet, there was no way I could refuse his offer. The mystery, the bizarreness of it all—it consumed me. Danger awaited, and though I wanted nothing more than to escape the fate of this nightmare, another part of me felt the need to see it through.

"Sure, Scott. Let's do that."

"Great," he said. Then he paused and fell deep in thought all of a sudden—like he knew he wanted to say something else, but couldn't find the words. I gave him a minute to finish; he said nothing.

"Scott, are you alright?"

With the slightest shake, he snapped back to reality and looked right into my eyes.

"It'll be great, Derek," said Scott, as if he knew reassurance was in order. "I'll make sure there's no trouble."

***

As we walked through Scott's front door, with its battered screen and flimsy wooden frame that seemingly trapped you as it snapped shut behind you, my worst fear was relieved. Scott's mother, who I expected to be standing right there in the kitchen, clouds of cigarette smoke circling her silk dress, was nowhere to be found.

I did not dare ask Scott where she was. But my feeling of relief was that I was able to walk through that kitchen without seeing anything that reminded me of what I had experienced four nights prior; it started the evening off in a positive light. I had been dreading another up close and personal encounter with that ghoulish eyesore ever since the plans had been made.

However, my sense of reassurance that Scott and I could hang out without any terror was a direct result of ignorance. My ignorance, to an important fact that would not have gone overlooked had I not been so distracted by my previous encounter...

There was still another adult living at that house.

***

I had managed to block out most of the paranoia that cycled through my brain by around 8:00 PM. My focus progressed toward simply having a nice night with my friend, and I was cruising. On top of that, still no sign of Scott's mother...

I live with my dad, Derek. My mother died when I was two.

The thoughts came and went; I did my best to ignore them. The night had actually been fun due to Scott being in such great spirits. We played football in the backyard, we ordered pizza, and we talked about an upcoming school project we planned to work on together. I began to feel how I remembered feeling with my friends back in Buford.

Though, something odd occurred a bit earlier before any of the fun started. When we first walked into Scott's room after passing through the kitchen, I instantly noticed something that was missing. It wasn't something I had expected to recall so easily, but it still stood out.

"Hey, where are your turtles?" I asked, half-expecting him to have a good answer right away. He didn't.

In response to my question, I hadn't noticed Scott drift off in thought the same way he had earlier in the week. I managed to point out that the metal pan filled with water for the turtles was missing as well, and then saw that Scott had a desperate, troubled look on his face; he was clearly attempting to come up with something to say.

"You know, it's pretty nice out," he muttered, almost more to himself than to me. Lifting his head nervously, he looked at me with uncomfortable eyes. "Let's play some football!"

"Okay," I said. I followed him to the backyard, attempting to keep up, as his uneasy strides propelled him down the hallway toward the side door of the kitchen. The change of subject and sudden urge to exit the house was awkward and concerning; I forced myself to disregard it.

74

So the night progressed toward normalcy after that. What we did became a most enjoyable distraction and an excellent display of a burgeoning friendship. And, sure enough, *The Terminator* had just started on HBO as Scott and I huddled near the edge of his bed, a junky old television flickering in front of us. The dim and fading light of the screen produced a creepy glow that barely illuminated the pitch-blackness of the room.

Twenty minutes into the film, the sound of terror roared over the low volume coming from the television set. It was a familiar sound, but the repetition sent me into a traumatizing flashback. That snapping sound of the screen door was like a siren for the end of the world.

I shot a rapid glance over at Scott as the treacherous storm of footsteps began across the kitchen floor and continued into the hallway immediately thereafter. The roaring stomps echoed closer and closer toward his door.

"Shit, Derek..."

The look of fear in my friend's eyes pierced my heart, and I felt my stomach drop as I tried to balance my fear with the care I felt for him. Our eyes locked, and both of us, instinctively, jumped to our feet and headed straight for the bedroom window.

The barging of footsteps viciously transformed into the pounding of the door; each hit landed like a crash of thunder that shook the entire house.

"Shit, it wasn't enough," Scott said to himself, as he pried open the window and began to hoist himself out.

I felt the chilling breeze of the evening as I followed him, the brightness of the moon beckoning me as I stared straight up toward it. The night was fresh, and the sky recently darkened to signify our safety was in jeopardy.

"Scott!" I called out as my friend sprinted toward the river bank.

"It wasn't enough," Scott yelled, barely audible enough for me to hear, "he needs more."

I caught up to him right as he knelt at the pebble formation on the bank. The distant sound of thunder rumbled as a threatening wind began to surround us.

"Ronnie, I'm so sorry," Scott said, reaching inside a small pipe stuck out from an incline in the bank. It looked like it was about a foot in diameter, and I could see tiny creatures crawling around inside.

The rest are over by the river...

"Sam and Bridget?" I asked him, "Is this where Sam and Bridget went?"

"They're gone. They weren't enough," he said, scrambling to scoop up one of the other turtles inside. "There's barely any left. They stopped coming."

Lightning struck, cracking the sky in half and illuminating the backyard so I could see the terror that faced us near the house. He was like the Incredible Hulk, but merely a silhouette of a looming, destructive figure. He, *it*, was the man from the hallway.

"SCOTTYYYYY!!!" he roared with intense hostility, though his voice became lost in the thunder.

Scott held the turtle out toward the direction of his father, whispering to the creature as he clutched it softly in both hands. "I'm so sorry, Ronnie..."

The silhouette advanced toward us in yard-long strides, on stomping legs that appeared bigger than tree trunks. The moist soil squished beneath his work boots; each imprint was more unsettling than the last as they drew nearer. Within seconds, he was standing right before us, and all I could see was the shape of his massive dark form and two gleaming, red eyes: Two furious floating circles fixated directly on prey.

He violently snatched the turtle out of Scott's hands. The force of his aggression felt like a wave of punishment in front of me.

"Dad, don't—" but Scott's plea had zero effect. Nothing could stop what came next.

I watched in horror as the head of poor Ronnie disappeared into the jaws of that menacing beast. With a series of chomps and an apathetic snarl to follow, Scott's father gazed down at his son, victorious. After an exaggerated swallow, chewed-up bits of flesh and skull inched their way down his throat.

Scott turned his head toward the ground, refusing to watch the decapitated reptile's blood drain from its underbelly into the second bite of his father's fangs. I couldn't turn away as Ronnie's body shriveled beneath its shell. When the last of its remains were sucked dry, Scott's father apathetically tossed the shell onto the rocks. It produced an awful clunking sound as it bounced into the water.

"YOU...MUST...ALWAYS..."

Scott looked up again, tears streaming down his cheeks as rain began to fall from the sky.

"...FEED...THE...MASTER..."

"I tried, Dad—"

"ENOUGH!" he bellowed, swiftly turning around and storming back toward the house. The whole Earth shook beneath every demonizing step until he was gone.

"What just happened?!" I cried. "What was that?!"

"Go home, Derek," Scott said, his face staring toward the slippery rocks on the bank, "and don't come back again."

He was no longer crying, not even a whimper. "Go home, Derek," he repeated.

"Scott..."

He ignored me, and picked himself up off the ground, running swiftly back toward the house. I didn't know what to think, or say. But in the aftermath of less than five seconds of utter confusion, I was the only person left outside.

As I paced forward in the direction of my home, I felt an unspeakable combination of confusion, terror, loneliness, and defeat, and then I saw that someone else was there. Her blank face just stared out through the kitchen window, without so much as the slightest movement or shift in composure as I walked right past.

***

Over the next few days, I saw Scott at school like always. We acknowledged each other with brief eye contact but did not speak to one another; our only reactions were a slight head nod here and there. I noticed there was something a little different about him, something I could not quite

77

decipher. It almost seemed as if there was an absence of sadness in him that I had never seen before.

It didn't make sense to me, given the horrific incident I had witnessed that recent evening. But as our brief friendship came to a halt and dissipated into nothingness, it seemed as if his troubles faded and that he was consistently content. It was as if nothing had ever happened.

I sometimes walk by Scott's house during the day and revisit the river bank where that pipe housed some of his turtle friends. I'm careful to look around and make sure that Scott, along with that treacherous beast that chased him out into the backyard and that faceless woman in the kitchen window, is nowhere to be found. But to this day, I've never seen another turtle by the river.

In the past, I've seen two therapists and both did a great job of listening, yet I always wondered if they believed what I was telling them. Call it paranoia, call it neurosis if you will—but any time I shared a personal experience, be it traumatic, euphoric, or even questionable, I felt an intense desire to come across as truthful. Then I started to realize it wasn't the therapists' job to trust me, it was their job to earn my trust so they could help me trust myself. From there, I started to wonder how often patients of psychology told lies to nurture their delusions. What would be the point of that if the end goal was to receive help? But then it started to make sense to me that internal peace would still be internal peace at the end of the day regardless of how one achieved it.

FOUR SESSIONS IN

"Before we go into that, I'd like to know more about the relationship it-self. If that's okay with you, of course."

Janet Greene tightened up; she always anticipated something like this was coming. Yet she wasn't simply nervous at the request for details. No, this was a slight tension related to the uncertainty of where to begin.

Sandy Mensforth had asked for these details once before, but Janet de-flected in an effort to dive into deeper territory both too fast and too soon. From Sandy's perspective, a new approach was needed to move for-ward.

After a moment of silence from her client, she intervened, "We don't need to talk about anything that makes you uncomfortable," Mensforth con-tinued, "I just feel this would be a helpful place to start."

"That's just the thing, Sandy. I don't know where to start," Janet admit-ted, her brows lifting with eagerness, "is there anything specific you'd like to know about...about me?"

The therapist had realized there was a peculiarity to how Janet attempt-ed to steer their conversations at times. She maintained a sort of con-trol with abrupt subject changes or intentionally vague requests, like she wasn't quite confused, or stuck at all, but attempting to challenge her support system in lieu of allowing it to challenge her. Or, maybe Janet was just in need of a companion to talk with due to some sort of boredom or loneliness and simply did not seek the help she claimed. These were not necessarily incorrect reasons for seeking therapy but there were moments where, despite having trained for all sorts of things over the past forty-five or so years, Sandy Mensforth still found herself stumbling over her next words in response to Janet's undeniable quirks.

Then again, there had been other moments thus far where Janet would not only follow her therapist's lead but open up willingly; it was as if she couldn't help herself. This behavior typically occurred after Janet's failed attempts at asking her own open-ended questions.

"How about this, what is the biggest obstacle in you and Theo's marriage? What's the first thing that comes to mind?"

"We can't seem to communicate," Janet said, without any hesitation. "No matter what we seem to say to one another, someone is always offended, or hurt, or even just annoyed. It's exhausting."

"Mmmhmm. Yes, I understand."

And then there was silence again.

"That's among the most common problems marriages face," the therapist added. "While I know what you're experiencing can be excruciating, you aren't alone."

"Yes," Janet said, softly. "I know."

"Are you able to share an example?"

"I can," Janet said. "But first, is there anything you'd like to know about me? My background, perhaps?"

As the pattern became increasingly apparent, Mensforth avoided feeding into the mind games her client was attempting to play. "You have the floor, Janet. Please, feel free to continue as you see fit."

Janet winced, then she paused. She looked at the floor for a few seconds, then lifted her head back up to make direct eye contact with Sandy again.

"Just this morning," she began, "Theo and I were having breakfast, like we always do; it was about 9:00 AM. I got up to get more coffee, and he grunted the moment I sat back down; it was not just a clearing of the throat, but a genuinely disgusted grunt."

Mensforth listened, as her client provided the details she knew would help lead this conversation to somewhere productive.

"I asked him if he was okay. He barely looked up, but said 'Of course, Jan, of course everything is fine. Why wouldn't it be?' and I could just hear his sarcasm, and the passive aggressiveness in his tone. It made me so upset, and when I told him that, he suddenly seemed angry.'"

"And then what?"

"Then he said, 'Seems a little odd, doesn't it? That you'd get more coffee without even offering me some? You can clearly see my cup is nearly empty, can't you?'"

"How did that make you feel?" the therapist asked after Janet came to a pause.

"I wanted to murder him," Janet said. There was no change in intensity as she spoke, rather she seemed indifferent when describing the feeling. "I was enraged, and I got up and stormed out of the kitchen."

"That is a very understandable reaction to have when being spoken to that way," Mensforth affirmed.

"So yes, Sandy, it's just a lot of little things like that. We are always bickering, it seems. Always pissing eachother off."

More silence. Mensforth waited patiently.

"You see, we've been married for about a year and a half now and things were great at first, during like the first five or six months. But then we started getting on each other's nerves, and then we started resenting each other for these random things, and now it's gotten to the point where I feel like I hate him half of the time. Like, I feel like I don't even know who I married."

"When did you first notice those feelings, the hatred?"

"Recently," Janet continued, "in the last month or so. I've felt these very dark and scary feelings towards him. Fantasies—violent ones, even."

"Now that we've come back around to this, let's go into it; tell me about the fantasies."

Janet paused, raising her brows with that same playful eagerness. "You want to know about my fantasies? How about how Theo and I first met?"

Mensforth avoided showing her frustration and kept a straight face—she even attempted showing consideration where there really wasn't any that she wanted to display at this point: "I'd like for you to continue how you'd like to; I always ask questions based on what information I feel would be helpful to know."

There was another moment of silence as Janet stared at the floor; she was suddenly less eager to go into the subject she had been so adamant about pursuing. Mensforth did not say another word.

"Sometimes I think about killing him," Janet said, softly, meeting her therapist's gaze again. "I think about it every day lately."

"Do you enjoy thinking about it?"

"I do and I don't," Janet said, "I feel better sometimes, after pondering what it would be like. And then there are other times where I get very sad and don't feel better at all; it's half and half most of the time."

"I see," Mensforth said; she was beginning to empathize further with her client. "When you imagine killing Theo, do you think about doing anything specific?"

"Always," Janet said with a hint of pride in her tone. After an awkward pause, she backpedaled, "Well, no, not really anything specific."

"You've described this as a fantasy," Mensforth stated, "how would you define that word, 'fantasy'?".

"I'd say...a 'fantasy' is something I think about doing sometimes, but wouldn't actually do most of the time," Janet said. She pondered the question further and started scratching her chin, like a thoughtful child.

From the middle of their first session and up until this very moment in their fourth session, Mensforth noticed an inconsistency in Janet's personality. She seemed to flow in and out of different traits, and it was difficult to gauge which version of her client she was speaking to, sometimes from moment to moment. It was a different subject for a different day, but it was constantly in the back of the therapist's mind thus far.

"That sounds right—please, continue."

"When he makes me angry or upset, I think about killing him. Not in any particular way, I guess. Maybe shooting him, or hitting him with some sort of object. I guess the basic ways to kill someone, you know?"

"I think I do," Mensforth said, showing no discomfort. "At this point in our conversation, Janet, I have to ask, do you ever consider acting on these fantasies?"

"I could never hurt Theo," Janet said, with a genuine compassion and loving tinge to the way she spoke. "I'll admit, I sit and I think about how I can express this anger and this hatred I feel towards the way he is sometimes. And I hate myself sometimes for even thinking about it. But I just feel angry."

Janet's replies were scattered. Mensforth had noticed they sometimes seemed uncertain, and the subject seemed to make Janet uncomfortable. Other times, the information was provided with such precision and was so well-articulated that it almost came across as rehearsed.

"Sometimes, Janet? What about the other times? Do you hate yourself those times?"

"No, I don't hate myself; I just feel free."

"Tell me more about that feeling."

"It feels good to allow myself to think about doing something so extreme. To hurt the person I love—or once had stronger feelings of love for, I guess; those are the times I feel better afterwards."

"I can validate that," Mensforth said. "We tend to have a lot of thoughts, and they are not always positive. At the end of the day, a thought is only as harmful as the actions that result from it."

"I agree!" Janet said, with a sudden spark of enthusiasm enhancing her tone.

Despite the oddities surrounding Janet's personality, Sandy Mensforth had seen it all throughout her career. Having acquired the better part of five decades' worth of experience, the therapist had assisted clients who were determined to harm themselves or others. She knew who she was dealing with. There was no doubt that Janet's words could not be fully trusted; there were too many inconsistencies. But at her client's core, there was merely an insecure woman facing a period of uncertainty.

"What do you make of all this, Sandy?" Janet said, her tone shifting toward slight panic, absent of any sort of confidence that might've peppered their conversation thus far.

It was 7:57 PM; the session was just nearing its end.

"Well, Janet, you have stated that you have no intention to harm Theo. I think that's a great start. These feelings you are experiencing, while I might describe them as morbid, they are very common and tend to occur in unhealthy relationships. Try not to let your thoughts frighten you. Instead, I'd like for you to continue working towards improving your marriage—at the end of the day, you live together and want to be happy. That has always been your main goal, right?"

"Yes, Sandy; that's still all I want."

"Let's pick this back up next week," Mensforth said, donning a compassionate smile. "In the meantime, I want you to please reach out to me if you feel like your thoughts are making you uncomfortable and you need to talk through them; I am just a phone call away. There is no need to schedule an appointment."

"Thank you, Sandy."

And with that, Janet picked up her purse and walked quietly out of Mensforth's office.

On her way home, a song came on the oldies station—it was "Walking On Sunshine" by Katrina and the Waves—and Janet sang it, loudly. The song always brought her back to when she was a kid, riding in her mother's station wagon. At that moment, she felt free; it was a sense of freedom coming from positivity and not from violent fantasies of murdering her husband. There was a relief from the pain and stress over what she had confessed to Mensforth during their session. Janet was experiencing an eagerness to arrive back to the house and see Theo. She felt excitement as she thought about pursuing the happy marriage she and Theo had begun just a year and a half prior.

***

"Hi, Honey," Janet said as she walked through the front door, plopping her bag down onto the couch in the living room. Dark, musky, and chilly, their dwelling would seem desolate to random visitors; to Janet, it was home.

Theo stared straight forward, eyes wide open, offering no response. Janet looked back at him, with a slight frown on her face, and turned toward the kitchen.

"Therapy went great! Thanks for asking," she said, sarcastically. Despite Theo's lack of response, she had no intention of starting an argument. His silence protested Janet's bubbly positive energy and filled the other room with contention; this was made all the more clear as Janet opened the door to the refrigerator.

"You're not too talkative," Janet said, walking back over to the living room with a can of Diet Coke in hand. His silence continued, and Janet began to sneer at him. The unrelenting absence of dialogue from her partner blended perfectly with the muted TV screen across from him playing one of his favorite episodes of "The Rifleman."

"Sandy and I already started to break some ground tonight," Janet continued, "and we are only four sessions in! We talked about you and I's relationship a bit. But mostly, I'm just feeling like things are going to be just fine with us...*Dear*," Janet said, chuckling to herself. "But if I'm going to make it to my pottery class in the morning, I better get some sleep—I'm beat!"

With that, Janet leaned over to the side table next to the living room couch and kissed the glass jar sitting atop it. Inside the jar, Theo's eyes remained wide open, continuously staring ahead; the formaldehyde surrounding his head glistened in the light from the nearby lamp. Janet hummed the chorus to "Walking On Sunshine" quietly to herself and started towards the stairs leading to their bedroom, flipping off the light on her way out.

I sometimes find "true crime" to be an insult to injury. It is almost as if we already secretly feel the shame and guilt of being entranced by the atrocities of human nature—but now, let's surpass making up our own stories, and indulge in someone else's real-life pain as a means to entertain us. Needless to say, it's not a guilt that many would ever own. It is an accepted part of what is, in my opinion, our nasty, American culture; not at all unlike our callous consumption of processed meats or our participation in the stock market. At the end of the day, we are all just pawns in a filthy system.

When I wrote the following story, obdurately different in format than the others in this collection, my vision more matched an X-Files episode rather than a serial killer documentary on streaming—I'll let you decide.

ANITA

5/27/2014 - 8:32 PM

My second week on the job and they handed me my first case. Believe me, I know what I signed up for in homicide; I know it's rough out here in L.A., I've lived here all my life. I followed most of my father's cases, even when I was a kid—and he was very discreet about his work. I always knew how fucked up this county was, and I always knew what he was dealing with. I knew how numb he was to all of the violence—this hatred, this suffering that never seems to go away. I knew what was coming when I took this job.

Still, I assumed I'd start out with something a little more basic. When you go from writing traffic tickets to filing robbery reports to chasing down criminals...Sure, now it's time to start solving murders. Though, as bizarre as they get, there are still plenty of basics out there. Drive-bys or bad drug deals were most of what you'd find on any day. Hell, even a crazed ex might be involved. All of those cases tend to make sense; they can be categorized into crimes of reason, regardless of how irrational. But a murder-suicide with no known motive and no history of mental illness, not even an inkling of instability—fuck; this one's a bit complicated. I meet the first *and only* "witness" tomorrow morning.

My family always makes fun of me for being naive, and this is what they're talking about. Jeanine, bless her, told me to "get right in there and go for it."

Apartments are interesting to me because you can live ten feet away from someone and know less than nothing about them. But when you grow up in a suburban home, your neighbors all the way down the street can easily become your best friends for life; they are nearly twenty times the distance from you, yet can be a thousand times closer. Communal urban living may easily result in isolation, and I've seen it a bunch already. What was it that Morgan Freeman said in *Seven*? Oh yeah, "In any major city, minding your own business is a science..."

Mrs. Davis claimed she didn't know a thing about Daniel Wright or his fiance, but definitely heard some unsettling noise at around 2:00 AM on the night of the murder. She said that, at first, it was the sound of a woman screaming in pain, then it was an even more intense scream, from a man; it seemed to her that it was a scream of anguish. Mrs. Davis knocked and knocked, but she only heard rummaging and footsteps in response. There was no answer, even after she had yelled for Danny to open up, and then there was dead silence.

"They seemed very happy," she told me. But there wasn't much to go off, considering Mrs. Davis admitted over and over again that she had spoken not more than three or four words at a time to either of her neighbors in the two years they lived across the hall from her.

I interviewed Danny's mother later in the afternoon. It broke my novice heart to hear her answer my questions through her whimpering and sobbing; it was a tough conversation indeed. There are many more of these sorts of interactions that have yet to come, for sure.

She, too, confirmed that her son and his fiance, Lauren, were very happy together. They bickered like a married couple and occasionally had a rough patch, but it was all typical relationship drama in her opinion, and it made her happy to see her son in such a good relationship. While he was never "Mr. Popular" in high school, her son managed to date around a bit in college, and eventually, Lauren Kepnick was "the one."

Aside from his parents going through a divorce when he was age eleven, an amicable and healthy split according to the mother, all signs point to a regular, boring, yet still personable guy with good relationships on all sides. With that said, he was not your average candidate for a brutal stabbing followed by an intentional sleeping pill overdose; nor was he one for an odd suicide note on the floor near the bodies: "To those who will experience pain as a result of my actions tonight, please understand I was void of choice. This world's treacherous winds have blown me away."

5/31/2014 - 4:47 PM

Memorial Day started with a department barbeque at Lieutenant Travis' place, an annual tradition I always heard about when working down the hall in theft. At around 4:00 PM, I heard news of another murder-suicide just four miles from Danny Wright's apartment; this time it was at a ranch in Culver City. There are other detectives in this department, but my boss is already hinting at putting me on this one, too. Two murder-suicides in the same week less than two miles from each other is not so common, apparently—not even in L.A.

Not what I signed up for.

5/31/2014 - 6:51 PM

Wholesome vibes from every corner of this residence. But of course, everybody has a dark side. How dark...well, it depends; it depends on a lot of different factors that I'm quite frankly not seeing anywhere here. Not after talking to the neighbors, not after doing a sweep of the house. And considering the more obvious shit—like the photos on the wall, the home decor, things like that—nothing points to this type of fate. There was nothing besides an open safe, which I can only assume housed the murder weapon—a Glock 19. But keeping a gun in the house for self-defense purposes is as common as anything else these days, and it was the only firearm found in the home. No obvious gun nuts were living here.

Katherine Wheeling was found dead on the living room couch, shot right through the side of her head, and there were three more bullets in her chest. The main suspect, her husband Jonathan Wheeling, was found in their shared bedroom; the Glock was still in his right hand, and his brains were splattered across the wall behind the bed. Mr. Wheeling was found lying on his back atop the queen-size bed, and the gunshot wound in the back of his head indicated that he had shot himself right through the throat. It was a nasty scene, an unsettling dichotomy of brutality against what seemed like excessively positive energy throughout the rest of the home.

To my point from a few days ago, the neighbors in this single-family community claim to have been much closer to the Wheelings. Jerry Marks, the old man next door, said Jon and Kate regularly went out to parties and clubs, that Jon was a graphic designer downtown, and that the two of them had mentioned wanting to have a child soon. Diane and Keith Lang, the younger couple two houses down, said they regularly invited the Wheelings over for game night, including dinner and wine. "They got along and occasionally argued, but it was really normal from what we could tell," Diane told me. "Kate and I were friends and she vented to me about their fights sometimes. They weren't perfect but it was never anything beyond typical marital issues."

I can't wrap my head around this one. I'm gonna have to dig deeper into the Wheelings. There must be more to them.

5/31/2014 - 9:02 PM

It's 9:00 PM and I've just finished going through medical records, not just Jonathan and Katherine Wheeling's, but combing through Danny Wright's and Lauren Kepnick's again as well. All of them were clear, with no mental or physical conditions beyond Jon's frequent sinus infections that led to ocular migraines. His most recent check-up revealed no ongoing concerns and nothing within the realm of symptoms that could lead to insanity. "Healthy as a horse," as they say.

I just hope I have all my ducks in a row right now. I never thought I'd be investigating a murder-suicide this early into the job—let alone two.

6/3/2014 - 4:58 PM

Two more bodies were found this morning. Now I have a third "murder-suicide" added to my plate. It's the third in a five-mile radius in less than two weeks, and Captain Drecklin is now considering them all as part of one investigation—*my* case. "Thirty-three years in this precinct and I've never once seen this," he told me. "Nothing even comes close; we most likely have a serial killer on the loose." I couldn't believe what I was hearing, and neither could he from what I could tell.

They're assigning me a partner, a second-year C.I. named Cal Hyung— we're about to head over to our first interview. He's always been nice to me so we'll see how this goes. I was really hoping to choose a partner on my own accord after I took on a few of these solo, but Drecklin insists I stay on this case because "You'll never learn this shit by taking it slow." If he's suggesting that I can handle a tough one as long as I'm not working alone, I might agree with him.

6/3/2014 - 7:03 PM

The last person to see these two alive was the maid. Not a live-in maid, but at last, someone Cal and I could talk to who actually knew the victims closely. The first thing I noticed was Cal's obvious observation method. He'd let me do the talking and questioning without as much of a peep coming from him. He offered his condolences to the maid before we left in a dry, monotonous tone. That was it.

Her name is Brenda Hadley, and she had stuck around that night to care for the woman, Cynthia Goode, who apparently had a headache. It wasn't until Alan Goode, Cynthia's husband, called her at 10:05 PM during his drive home, from a party he attended that night, that Brenda was relieved of her duty and decided to head out. She left just before Alan's arrival back to the house. And then the murder took place, supposedly.

So Brenda claimed she didn't witness shit—not a thing. But Alan had returned from a night out only to murder his wife in cold blood with a kitchen knife at some point that evening. He took that same knife and stabbed himself right through his abdomen sometime thereafter and the maid found both bodies at 8:00 AM the next morning. That's how it appears, at least. For any isolated incident, a murder weapon found in the husband's hand with only his prints all over everything would clearly spell out this hunch. But Drecklin is on my ass about a homicide suspect, insisting that these statistics simply don't correlate with how often murder-suicides occur in Los Angeles County. Cal, in his few words, agrees. I think I do, too, but I wish I didn't. And as sweet as Brenda seems to be, we now have our first possible suspect.

6/4/2014 - 2:57 PM

I made a rookie mistake, fortunately it was one that Cal caught this afternoon and is helping me cover so Drecklin doesn't chew me out. "Just blame it on forensics, the captain will never bother talking to them," he said.

A key piece of evidence was found at the scene of the second murder. It was one I hadn't even looked at during my initial follow-up with the crime scene investigators and I must've missed it during my sweep. It was a suicide note that was lying on the floor in front of the bed that Jon Wheeling's body was found on. This note had the exact message as the one found at the Wright residence. Word for word, it read: "To those who will experience pain as a result of my actions tonight, please understand I was void of choice. This world's treacherous winds have blown me away."

And, unsurprisingly, Cal found the same note at Alan Goode's place during his sweep. We've submitted all three notes to the FDEs to determine any similarities in handwriting.

6/5/2014 - 9:16 AM

Didn't sleep the last two nights. I'm officially stressed the fuck out...I've got nothing. The front desk clerk in Brenda's apartment complex confirmed to police yesterday morning that Brenda came home at 10:12 PM the night of the murder; it was just seven minutes after the phone records showed her call with Alan took place. That's right around the same amount of time it would take to travel there by car from the Goode residence, at least according to Google Maps. She could technically still be guilty, as Alan *could have* returned immediately after calling her, and then...

Well, up next is a lie detector test for Ms. Hadley to make sure that wasn't the case. But I can say right now, with the little experience I have with this shit, she's not the one we're looking for.

And on top of that, the Goodes are clean. *Were* clean, I should say. No criminal records. No history of mental health issues. Just another two casualties in this bizarre string of gruesome deaths. I won't deny that a psychopath is on the loose, a smart one at that—the three matching suicide notes guarantee it. I just don't want to believe some whacko is out there. How in hell are Cal and I going to catch this guy?

6/5/2014 - 3:43 PM

Cal agrees that Brenda is innocent. He said he knew it immediately—something about being able to read people like the back of his hand. But after that, he didn't say much else. We had still barely gotten to know each other. Just this afternoon, however, he showed off his experience even further and suggested we take a look further into the party, the one that Alan had supposedly been on his way home from. I hadn't even thought of that. It made me feel lucky to have a partner in this. Truthfully, I found relief once Drecklin put Cal on this case with me; I just hadn't felt that presence until now.

All Brenda could tell us was that the party was "somewhere in the Arts District downtown", at least that is what she thought Alan had said. Using phone tracking records, we could see where Alan was from 6:38 PM to 9:47 PM the night of the murder; he was at some building right in the heart of the Downtown Los Angeles Arts District, just like Brenda had said. So, Cal did some research and found out what had been going on at that address. Thank God for the internet.

6/5/2014 - 6:03 PM

We were able to quickly meet up with Tiffany Leung, the host of the art show that took place at the Ariti Gallery that night—the art show that, unless his phone was stolen, Alan Goode had attended for around three hours. When Cal demanded a list of everybody who signed in at the event, Ms. Tiffany seemed a bit put off. Granted, Cal has a serious and intimidating presence; I can't imagine the poor young girl was expecting to have to produce such a list without being asked any prerequisite questions. I had to avoid even the slightest smirk when I, too, was caught off guard by how brashly Cal made the demand, after not even a hello or any other pleasantries. We got the list. The event was *invite-only*, which made our next task a little simpler. Now the two of us had to interview twenty-three different people, just to see if they noticed anything significant or odd about Alan Goode that night.

Drecklin called me into his office right before I was about ready to head home for the day, asking for any leads on the "So Cal Suicide Killer." I told him a half-truth, that Cal and I were onto something. On top of all that, Brenda Hadley passed her lie detector test with flying colors. Though she still can't be completely ruled out as a potential suspect given her location at the time of the murders, we really don't have anything else on her.

6/6/2014 - 7:49 PM

Cal and I were able to get through eleven people between the two of us today; I spoke to five on my own and we spoke to three together. I swear, speaking to these intellectual art-lover types and MFA students felt like the world was in slow motion. It was not that they needed to be particularly upbeat, especially since a few of them did happen to know Alan Goode, but I've never sifted through a duller group of pretentious hacks in my entire life. I can just imagine how quickly the other three interviews went with Cal, though. There's something so coldly professional about his approach to this job from what I've witnessed so far. He's respectful and nice to me, but I almost get a vibe of contempt when I see him interviewing, like there's zero time for bullshit. He's not wrong.

Out of everybody we spoke to today, eight had no idea who Alan Goode was, even when we provided the most recent photograph of him. The other three we interviewed knew him from other gallery shows but didn't recall anything other than exchanging quick head nods or sharing a moment of brief critique about a photograph or two. We had nothing at all to help with our case, not from my end or Cal's. There are twelve more interviews to go, and they'll be done by the end of the week, hopefully.

6/7/2014 - 4:42 PM

Cal and I sort of made some headway today, and I'm really glad it was during one of the interviews we met up together for. Out of the seven people who attended the gallery show that we were able to talk to today, one person by the name of Hashim Singh had gone to photography school with Alan and agreed to meet up with him at the show. He broke down in tears during the interview, to which I noticed a slight twitch in Cal's left eye accompanied by a hint of a frown, showing just enough subtle empathy to disprove my partner's stoic demeanor.

According to Hashim, he had met a girl early on in the evening and they had started talking, which resulted in him speaking very little to Alan that night. But Hashim had noticed that Alan met somebody too, a considerably older woman with whom he appeared involved in a deep conversation for almost the entire time he was there. "At least an hour—or maybe even two", he said. By the time Hashim and his new lady friend were ready to leave the show together, Alan had seemingly already left without saying goodbye—no sign of the older woman anymore, either. And that was that. When I asked Hashim what his thoughts were on the recent tragedy, all he could do was sadly shake his head and say, "I don't know how he could do this. It doesn't make any sense."

Hashim further described the older woman as having curly, brown, graying hair and dark, thick-rimmed glasses. So far we've interviewed eighteen of the twenty-three "invite-only" guests and no one fits that description. Now I think we have to go back and ask them all more questions.

6/7/2014 - 8:34 PM

Miraculously, we were able to get through the rest of the five guests throughout the remainder of tonight. I'm fucking exhausted, but I'm feeling the rush. We might be getting closer to something here.

None of the five knew Alan, but all of them recalled seeing the older woman with curly, brown, graying hair and dark, thick-rimmed glasses. They all reported that they had wondered, albeit only briefly, who in the hell she was. Three out of the five people we interviewed also looked at the photo of Alan Goode and "thought they might've recalled" seeing the two of them speaking to each other for a while. But now we've interviewed everybody that was supposed to be at this party—again, invite-only—and we have definitely not spoken to this mystery lady. It's time to touch base with Tiffany Leung again. We'll try to get to her in the morning.

6/8/2014 - 6:13 PM

Tiffany got defensive when we asked who the older woman was, considering she was clearly not on the invite list. She told us she was "extremely busy that night," and that "people sneak into these types of things all the time; it's not like a VIP event at the White House." I tried to remind her that we were just trying to get as much information as we could, while Cal rolled his eyes and ended the conversation quickly. Afterward, he told me that reactions like that were only a red flag *if* the person was critical to the case details and that, in this circumstance, Tiffany Leung was not suspect. Cal said, "She's just a self-absorbed college student who thinks she's more important than she is." I'm still not ruling it out as suspicious.

The FDE department also got back to us. The handwriting for all three suicide notes that were found matches their corresponding victims. Our killer is either a genius at forgery, or they forced every one of their victims to write the same note.

6/9/2014 - 6:32 PM

We went back and interviewed most of the art show attendees again. None of them knew who the older woman was, but all of them remembered seeing her. A few of them changed their story once they got a chance to glance at the photo of Alan again, stating they "sort of remembered seeing the two of them talking."

6/10/2014 - 4:26 PM

Got through the rest today. Same results as yesterday.

A mysterious older woman sneaks into an art show and strikes up a conversation with a man who murdered his wife later that night. The phone records indicate no further correspondence between Alan and anyone other than Brenda, the maid. We've still got nothing, less than nothing. It appears the entire week has been a waste of time.

Drecklin is going to have to be patient with this one.

6/14/2014 - 11:13 PM

Another murder has been added to my case. And just when I thought we were headed towards a cold case after half a week of quiet.

Last night around 1:30 AM, a pick-up truck veered off Malibu Canyon Drive, crashed through the railing along the edge of Malibu Bluffs Park, and plummeted down the steep hill behind it, killing Jason Hodges, a thirty-one-year-old male from Topanga, and his partner of eight years, Samantha Flynn, age twenty-eight. Jason was behind the wheel; tire tracks showed the trek off-road in the direction of the hill. Forensics therefore determined the whole act was intentional as opposed to a freak accident.

Cal and I hit the scene right away, arriving earlier this afternoon, and discovered an invitation, miraculously still resting on the dashboard of the mangled truck, to a Norman Tech (assumingly Jason or Samantha's place of business) goodbye party for employee Kassie Moran at a sports bar called Touchdown Jim's. The date and time? Earlier that Sunday evening, June 13th at 9:00 PM. We looked into one party and there was no reason not to look into another at this point.

We also did a sweep of Jason Hodges' apartment in Topanga where he lived with Samantha, and found it was squeaky clean, except for the same recurring suicide note found on the kitchen table, once again in different handwriting. It read, "To those who will experience pain as a result of my actions tonight, please understand I was void of choice. This world's treacherous winds have blown me away." As unsettling as these notes are, at least we have a concrete way to determine which future incidents are part of this investigation and which of them are likely unrelated.

Jim's is closed on Mondays so we'll hit it in the morning. I was half-expecting Cal to reject my attempt to mirror his strategy, throw me a curveball, and suggest we interview Jason Hodges' family first. He didn't.

6/15/2014 - 1:32 PM

It's my job to act as if I am not fazed by anything that Cal or I might come across, but this case is getting stranger and stranger.

We stopped by Touchdown Jim's an hour before they opened for lunch this morning, 10:00 AM on the dot. The owner and bartender were almost finished pulling down the bar stools and they were no doubt surprised to see two detectives knocking on the locked entrance door, but were as cooperative as we needed them to be. Neither of them had worked two nights ago, so they didn't know a thing about the party, who set it up, and so on. The owner dug up an email from someone named Barbie Sampson who had reserved a section of the bar and submitted a head count. That really didn't tell us anything except the name of one person we could interview as soon as we got the chance. So the only thing left to do was watch the surveillance tapes for the evening of June 13th to see if we could notice anything of interest.

The footage was grainy and choppy, which made this point in the investigation especially tedious and excruciating. From what Cal and I could make out, there had been no altercations, no intense moments or arguments as far as I could tell, just some rowdiness and dancing over by the little karaoke station in the corner of the bar area. But we had our eyes on Jason Hodges, who we were nearly positive could be ID'ed from the recent photo we obtained yesterday. I tried to see how many drinks he had because maybe this whole thing was the result of drunk driving, but neither Cal nor I noticed him take so much as a sip of anything the entire night. All we noticed, and this was easy to detect because we had them both standing in one spot the whole time, was Jason talking to the same person uninterrupted for what the tape clock showed as roughly two hours and fifteen minutes. And from what we could make out, that person was an older-looking woman, with dark, curly hair and a pair of thick-rimmed glasses.

6/15/2014 - 6:33 PM

We tracked down Barbie Sampson via the same email address she used to contact the events coordinator at Jim's. She got back to us immediately and agreed to meet near Norman Tech during her lunch hour. She remembered seeing Jason talking to the older woman, thought it was odd, and confirmed this woman was "definitely not an invited guest" to Kassie's goodbye party she threw "for Norman Tech employees only."

"I assumed he had just met her somewhere else in the bar, randomly... you know how it is when you're out", is what Barbie said after stating the place was packed with other people outside of their little work function. Tearing up, she also told us that she couldn't believe this had happened to Jason and Samantha and that "Jace" was "one of the nicest guys she had ever worked with".

While heading back to the precinct, Cal looked at me and said he had never seen anything like this before. I told him "I still don't know what this *is* yet", to which he quietly replied, "Touche."

Seeing a visual of the older lady with the thick-rimmed glasses was truly haunting. I have no idea what significance she plays in these murders, but I'm afraid to find out. I keep hoping that four murder-suicide cases just aren't as unusual as Drecklin claims so that we can eventually rule out his theory of a "grand assailant." But the writing is on the wall at this point—I know I am just in denial.

6/18/2014 - 10:14 AM

Cal made a breakthrough in our case. Truly lucky I landed him as a partner in this mess.

After a full two days of reviewing evidence from the four murders, he found a ticket stub buried in the back of Daniel Wright's wallet for a *Pig Farm Romance* concert, some local L.A. experimental group. The show was at The Lucky Horse, a small club downtown, and it was on the same night he supposedly came home and murdered his fiance and offed himself at around 2:00 AM.

The surveillance footage from The Lucky Horse was much more high-tech and advanced than that of Touchdown Jim's. The whole thing took a while to access—we were getting what we needed, so I can't complain too much. Cal and I discovered what we expected, but we were no less disturbed by what we found: Daniel Wright, as clear as crystal from the photos we had, standing by the bar, having a nearly two-hour-long conversation with the woman who is now the prime suspect in our case.

An urgent department meeting with Drecklin is scheduled for 4:00 PM. Cal and I will push for a clip from the Lucky Horse surveillance tapes to be released on the eight o'clock news naming the unidentified older woman with the curly, brown, graying hair and thick-rimmed glasses as our suspect in the "So Cal Suicide Killer" case—and that she is wanted alive.

I can't believe it.

6/18/2014 - 9:32 PM

It's been a long week. I'm still in disbelief that the entire world now has a direct visual of our suspect. Los Angeles County has been instructed to join the manhunt by remaining on the lookout for this mysterious un-identified woman, and I feel like I'm still the one with the most questions. Is she the killer? Is she linked to someone else who is the killer? Whoever is committing these murders has something to do with this woman. I've never been so spooked by a case in my entire life. I haven't gotten a good night's sleep in over six days and I don't think tonight is going to end that streak.

On top of all this, I got in a big fight with Jeanine tonight. I've been snap-ping at her left and right because I'm fucking miserable and tired. This isn't fair to her. I remember the same thing happening to my parents whenever my father was stuck on a tough case.

Dad, if you're reading this...help me crack this case. I don't think you ever dealt with anything this strange. But I know if you were alive today, you could do it.

6/19/2014 - 6:01 PM

Uneventful day today, aside from this morning when our story was run on every major network in the country. The nationwide search for the So Cal Suicide Killer has begun. Eight victims. One suspect. No name.

And so far, no reports.

6/20/2014 - 7:23 PM

Still no reports today. News stations are continuing to promote the man-hunt throughout the day. Cal and I have combed through the evidence to the ends of the Earth at this point and found nothing new. We were hop-ing to link our suspect to the murders of Katherine and Jon Wheeling, the second case, chronologically; but we still have just the other three. Unless that case is isolated, we can only assume it was her.

My eyes and ears are constantly in a state of red alert, but all we can do is wait now—whether that is looking forward to the first set of good news or anticipating more bad news.

6/20/2014 - 2:17 AM

Victim #9 was taken tonight, 26-year-old Reese Kendrick, and—I'm still in utter shock—his killer THOUGHT he had successfully taken his husband, Jack, too. The poor guy survived. Jack is currently alive and in intensive care at USC Arcadia Hospital. And if he pulls through, this could be a major stroke of luck for our case. *Major.*

I got the call a few hours ago, right after I had given up hope for the evening. Cal and I headed over to the Kendricks' condo in Silver Lake. Reese's death was made to look like a suicide, just like all the others. This time, a piece of broken glass was in the victim's hand and a shattered window was nearby, the victim's throat slit straight across; there was a real mess on the floor and walls of their spacious kitchen. And yet again, the same suicide note was lying on the floor nearby. That's five notes now with identical inscriptions. Jack was found nearly unconscious in the adjacent living room, beaten bloody and strangled within inches of his life. He was murmuring into the phone with the 911 operator still on dispatch. By the time we got there, Jack had already been taken away by the EMTs. An officer who got to the scene first told us that the trauma sustained around his esophagus, along with the internal bleeding from the beating, was enough to potentially end his life, post-ER admittance.

For all I know, Cal is still at the precinct doing his thing to get a head start on all the research we have on our plate. I'm completely exhausted and am not going to touch this any further until the morning. This city has taken too much out of me for one night.

6/21/2014 - 11:12 AM

Our first eyewitness report since the news bulletin finally came through this morning. A woman claimed she was fairly certain she saw our suspect speaking to a man at a party she was at last night—around 7:15 PM, roughly. Cal and I met with her right away. Cal's first question, which almost sounded more like a statement, and more blunt than I had yet heard from him: "Why didn't you report this sooner—are you aware that a person has been murdered, with another in critical condition?"

Anna Raleigh, the eyewitness, quickly stated that her son had broken his arm playing street hockey last night. She got the call to leave the party shortly after she had spotted our suspect and was unable to contact us at the time; she was then preoccupied the rest of the evening. Her story wound up checking out, and I believed her anyway. But had she gotten to us sooner, we might have been able to catch our killer as well as save a life—possibly two, God forbid Jack doesn't make it. The description Anna gave of the man she saw speaking to an old woman with thick-rimmed glasses, though? Lo and behold, a picture-perfect match with Reese Kendrick.

The pieces of this puzzle are starting to fit together now. We are so close.

6/21/2014 - 5:32 PM

As of this moment, Jack Kendrick has a 95% chance of survival. He will be inaccessible for at least another day or so while remaining in intensive care. The second we can speak to him, we will find out who did this.

6/24/2014 - 12:03 AM

I am in a state of complete delirium. I doubt I'll be able to get a moment of sleep tonight, and the last thing I want is to be up right now writing this entry. There is so much to document and I barely know where to begin.

First, we received a call from USC Arcadia at around 5:30 PM stating that Jack Kendrick pulled through and was stable enough for questioning. Cal and I were on our way until we got a second call straight from the precinct. A report had just come in that our suspect was spotted at a fundraiser in Fullerton speaking to a younger man that the caller happened to know. I got out of Cal's car and immediately caught a quick cab to the Fullerton Community Center in hopes of catching our killer and putting a stop to all of this; I arrived in just under ten minutes.

The initial report came from Dawn McKinley, a middle-aged member of OCPAC (Orange County Parents of Autistic Children), who agreed to discreetly meet me out front and escort me into the event undercover with an L.A.P.D unit close behind me. When I got there, Dawn came out and informed me that the older woman with curly hair and thick glasses had walked off and then disappeared from the event only moments earlier, but the man she was speaking to, a twenty-six-year-old man she knew from the community named Dirk Fowler, was still inside socializing.

My interview with Fowler was awkward, largely due to my inexperience in this field. I was frantic and adamant about getting answers, which is no way to approach a potential witness. Cal and I would have been better off switching for this one. Fowler came off surprised and, while fully willing to cooperate, only had nice things to say about his conversation with our suspect, a "nice older lady named Carolyn." According to him, they had initially discussed the fundraiser's goals and moved on to the topic of Dirk's younger brother, an autistic twenty-two-year-old, and what it was like growing up with a neurodivergent sibling.

He said they had talked for around an hour and a half, which is a long time to speak to one person at a community event. Yet, he seemingly found nothing strange about their interaction. I explained to Fowler that we would need to take him down to the station and process his official statement and that I would be placing him under close surveillance for at least 24-48 hours, given the circumstances of our case. While still confused and frazzled, Dirk continued to cooperate and was a good sport about being followed home by two police cars that would remain parked outside his residence.

Three other officers arrived at the fundraiser to begin questioning the other attendees. No other witnesses claimed to see where our suspect might've gone, but not a single one of them knew who she was, either. At an event like this, however, the woman's age did not stand out and she blended in easily, as many new faces tended to appear in support of fundraisers such as this one. The witnesses were of no help to our investigation, but being able to interview Dirk Fowler and obtain protection for him was a positive step forward.

With four officers staking out Fowler's home in nearby Buena Park, I left to go meet Cal at Arcadia around 7:45 PM. I got a chilling call from him while on my way there. Cal had only recently begun speaking to Jack and learned that his partner's death was, in fact, a suicide. Reese had been the one who had beaten and strangled him. There was no outside killer. No eyewitness of our suspect. It was an attempted murder followed by a real suicide. "I'm sorry, babe. I have to do this," were the last reported words Jack's husband said to him before the sudden and unhinged assault took place. And as Jack lay in the next room, clinging to the last minutes of his life, his blurred vision barely made out his husband writing the note and then taking his own life.

I keep replaying Cal's voice over and over again on that call: "Get your officers in that house. Get them in the house now." I dispatched a call over to the squad cars in front of Dirk Fowler's residence and informed them we had a 10-54 and to take Dirk and his partner into custody immediately. After no answer, the officers took down the door and found two more dead bodies. Dirk, unconscious in the downstairs hallway with a half-empty bottle of bleach found on the kitchen counter, and Dirk's long-time partner, Missy Kraus, lying still in the kitchen, appearing to have suffered multiple blows to the head from a slightly dented fire extinguisher that was found just feet away; it ended up having Dirk's fingerprints all over it. And, unsurprising to say the least, the same copycat suicide note was found.

I hate the realization that we could have prevented two more deaths. I also have no idea what to make of any of this. This is the most bizarre and unexplainable string of related cases I have ever known of. So much violence, all domestic... Regular people murdering their closest partners in cold blood...

I won't sleep tonight. I don't want to know what tomorrow might bring. I just want to hold Jeanine close and shut out the rest of the world.

6/24/2014 - 8:08 PM

I took a much-needed day off, but all I did was think about the case in every waking second. I'm discovering a painstaking challenge that is part of this job, one that is clearly driving me mad in obsession: I don't just seek to stop the people responsible for these murders and suicides, I seek to make sense of them. I remember my father's words when I was first starting to take an interest in this career path, they were among the last words he ever said to me: "Think like the killer so you can catch them, not so you can understand them. You will never understand them."

6/25/2014 - 7:32 PM

There have been no reports or incidents since Wednesday evening, the night of the Fowler-Kraus slaying. Cal and I spent all of today reassessing the case.

We have eleven dead and one survivor, an eyewitness who states our suspect was nowhere in sight during their partner's rampage. We have proof that the deaths of Victims #11 and #12 took place without our suspect anywhere in the area. We have six identical suicide notes, all with handwriting matched to each of the perpetrators. We have video evidence and numerous eyewitness accounts of an older woman speaking to five of the victims within hours of them murdering their partners and themselves. All locations where our suspect has been spotted, as well as all eleven deaths, have taken place within a ten-mile radius of one another.

And yet, still, all we have is a face. I don't know who we're looking for, or why.

6/26/2014 - 2:03 AM

The precinct received a call shortly after all the major networks ran their 10:00 PM news bulletin. The caller claimed to be related to the suspect. Cal and I immediately got in the car and went an hour north to an apartment complex in Palmdale.

Gale Burkhardt, a widow of age eighty-three, identified the suspect she saw on the news as Anita Miller, her cousin who was stabbed to death in 1991. According to Gale, Anita's husband, Michael Miller, was the only suspect named in the killing, but he was never captured, and he was never seen or heard from again. The photo of Anita that Gale provided was taken at the Venice boardwalk and dated two years before her death. Anita does resemble the image from our video surveillance footage semi-accurately, but due to the angle, I was unable to confirm a conclusive ID.

It is going to take some time to go through the records and validate Gale's statement. We need to dig a lot deeper because this simply isn't possible. A psychiatric evaluation for Gale will determine whether we are wasting our time.

6/26/2014 - 3:03 PM

Records for fifty-three Anita Millers came up in the California database for the past hundred years. Surprisingly, three of them died in 1991. But Cal was able to narrow those three reports down to only one murder.

Anita Miller was born in 1929 in Prescott, AZ, and died in 1991 in Venice Beach, CA; she was murdered at sixty-two years of age, just as Gale Burkhardt had said. A local Venice paper, which Cal managed to dig up, had a story on the murder that featured a photo of the victim. The image was a much more obvious match to our surveillance footage than the photo Gale provided. There she was, our suspect clear as crystal—with an eerie smile, curly, graying, brown hair, and dark-rimmed glasses—staring right back at me. My heart skipped a beat when I saw her; it was like she was on the other side of a window.

Cal had to remind me this whole thing was just a coincidence, that our suspect is not the deceased Anita Miller, and that Gale Burkhardt merely recognized the similarities when she saw the footage on the news and simply made a phone call. After all, at eighty-three years old, it was not such a shocking act for a lonely widow. Still, every little bit helps in an investigation—even when it doesn't seem useful.

We still don't have any other leads, though—living, or dead.

6/28/2014 - 9:08 PM

The rest of the weekend was quiet and followed by an uneventful Monday at the station sifting through evidence with Cal. We came up with nothing new: no more reports, no suspect sightings. More of my father's words haunt me as I suffer through this case: "The worst part about being a homicide detective is waiting for the next body to drop."

As of today, this case has been active for a full month.

6/29/2014 - 8:46 PM

We have her.

She is detained and awaiting interrogation. As of this moment, she is refusing to speak and hasn't spoken one word since the arrest. But she is in custody.

At around 12:30 PM today, we received a call that a mysterious older woman matching our suspect's description had shown up at an outdoor luncheon hosted by the overhead team at Shokiru, a fashion boutique based in downtown L.A. At first, none of the guests knew who she was or why she was there, but another employee noted that they had seen footage of the woman on the news and quickly made the call. Cal and I got there in less than twenty minutes with a full squad as backup. Every witness confirmed that our suspect had not yet spoken to anybody as she had been carefully avoided by the entire staff.

She remains unidentified. There was no ID on her at the time of arrest, and no other belongings were found on her. She refused to utter a single word when asked for her name, age, address, or why she was at the event. We know she is physically capable of speaking based on our surveillance footage and the few eyewitness accounts we have. This woman is carefully evoking her Fifth Amendment right by staying silent.

When it comes to our only suspect linked to this string of murder-suicides, there is currently nothing Cal or I can do until she agrees to cooperate. And we have no proof that she has done anything wrong, let alone illegal. Without any means to identify her, she will remain in custody.

6/30/2014 - 5:34 PM

Cal and I, along with Jay and Nico from homicide, rotated attempts to get our suspect to talk today. At around 2:00 PM, she broke her silence and I was the lucky candidate who got to hear her out.

She began, in a very quiet, frail voice, stating "I do not know why you have taken me in, and I wish to be released." I'll never forget the calmness and absence of hostility in her tone. She still refused to state her name. I began my questioning after stating that our department has proof of her speaking to several victims merely hours before they committed murder and suicide, which is why she is in custody and under questioning. To that, she replied, "I don't know anything about any suicides or murders, but I do enjoy socializing." I then asked her why she seemingly attended such a variety of events that she had been previously uninvited to, to which she replied, "Is it a crime to randomly explore the society and culture of Los Angeles?"

I used my training to redirect the conversation, in hopes of obtaining any information that might be useful later on. I asked her to tell me a little about herself, including her name—again, if she was willing. She let out a giggle that was frighteningly innocent-sounding and said, "Oh, I guess that couldn't hurt at this point. My name is Frances, Frances Albert. What else would you like to know?" I asked for her address, the reason she didn't have identification, and if she had any family or friends she wished to speak to—all of which she declined to answer. I asked her if she would please tell us anything that might explain why eleven people, five of whom she directly conversed with, are now dead. She repeated that she didn't know anything about that, but this time, added that "the world is a mysteriously treacherous place." We made deep eye contact when she said this, and my blood chilled. To say my heart skipped a beat would be an understatement. I experienced a terrifying jolt that seemed to transport me into a different realm. It was a hell I'm unwilling to go back to ever again, not even for a second or two.

She went on to willingly describe her hobbies: making jewelry, studying wildlife, and cooking. She claimed to have grown up near Albuquerque, NM, where she played on a softball team for most of her teenage years until a crippling knee injury all but destroyed that hobby forever. Her sadness by this was apparent, and there were other sad topics throughout the conversation: a past love who was killed in the army, a farmhouse owned by her mother and father that burned to the ground in a brush fire, and various shortcomings throughout her personal life. By this point, she flooded me with information I hadn't asked for and seemingly had no desire to stop.

She talked for over an hour and provided me with absolutely nothing that helped with our case. With Cal being, well, Cal—I'm half-expecting him to decipher something from the recording that will solve this thing once and for all.

6/30/2014 - 7:48 PM

To those who will experience pain as a result of my actions tonight, please understand I was void of choice. This world's treacherous winds have blown me away.

ACKNOWLEDGEMENTS

To my parents, for never batting an eyelash over my interest in morbid fantasy from such an early age. Most parents would have consulted a child psychologist after viewing some of my drawings from age 7, but they embraced my creativity and allowed me to express myself.

To my friends, Antonio Marquez, Nick Donahue, Aaron Ross and Drew Brown, and to my brothers, Kevin and Tim Hoffman, for reading the early drafts of these stories and offering kind words as motivation.

To my wife, Destynne, and my daughter, Grace, for providing unconditional love in an otherwise hateful world.

To Alvin Schwartz, R.L. Stine and Stephen King, for creating inspirational works of horror that helped shape me as a writer from my childhood, through my teenage years, and over the past twenty years of adulthood.

Last but not least, to my editor, Glenn S. Ritchey III, for joining forces to make this publication happen. Your unique ability to be both a friend and mentor during this process has changed my outlook on partnering with others to create works of art—for the better, of course.

John Hoffman has previously written for *Maximum Rocknroll*, *Revolver* and *Cvlt Nation*, and has been involved in the punk/ hardcore/metal scene since 1998. John has toured around the world as a vocalist for the hardcore band Weekend Nachos, and currently self-produces the doom metal band Stomach. He lives in Geneva, Illinois, a suburb of Chicago, with his wife Destynne and his daughter Grace. Besides writing and playing music, John enjoys all types of food and video games from the 80's and 90's. *Oil Spill* is his first book.